Hell Hath No Fury

WRATH

ANGELA ADDAMS

Wrath
ISBN # 978-1-80250-743-0
©Copyright Angela Addams 2024
Cover Art by Kelly Martin ©Copyright August 2024
Interior text design by Claire Siemaszkiewicz
Totally Bound Publishing

WRATH

Dedication

To Chaos… Cheers. You win.

Chapter One

Charlie

For a born werewolf, the full moon would bring nature into balance. A night filled with fun, games and satiation of all senses.

For a newly bitten werewolf, that very same bloom in the night sky would bring chaos, pain and often, especially for females, death.

I stared out through the floor-to-ceiling windows in the hallway just next to the guest suite and let the iridescent glow bathe me, soothe me, wash me of my sins.

You wish, my beastly darker half grunted, not so much in words as in scalding attitude.

Cynical bitch.

By the sounds coming from inside the room next to me, I knew that the worst of my sins was, in fact, wishing me dead this very moment.

I hoped Ruby would forgive me at some point so she could see that happen—my death, that was—when we were both into our two-hundreds and speckled gray old gals. We could die together, on the same day even, so we'd never have to feel the loss of one another's presence.

That was how I'd always envisioned best friends, found sisters, would live and die.

Never having had one in my life, I obviously got some things wrong.

For one, she was human...or had been less than three days ago, incompatible with my very—death to anyone human who knew—secret werewolf existence.

Two, before now, she had no idea that werewolves existed, because, well, as mentioned, it was immediate death to humans who knew that monsters of lore were, in fact, real.

Three, she was about to become one herself, which would likely kill her.

So yeah, best friends forever—but only if she survived the night. After that, I'd be grateful if she didn't hate me for more than a handful of decades.

With my bite, a powerful, werebeast alpha's bite, my best friend, my *now* pack-mate Ruby's transformation could go either way. I didn't know enough about how my werebeast bite would take to a female human. As far as I knew, it had only happened thousands of years ago when female warriors built armies of werebeasts like her, but those days had died long before I'd been born—so long ago, in fact, that their existence had been wiped from our shared history by the patriarchal alphas who ruled the clans today.

There was no current proof that what I'd done to Ruby in an effort to save her life would work out in a positive way. My beastly instincts said differently, maddeningly confident that this, too, would pass, that Ruby would rise and be stronger than she'd ever been as a human, a worthy and formidable soldier in my ever-growing army.

I could only hope for the best and put what little faith I had that my ancient beastly awareness knew what we were doing.

Ruby would only growl through gritted teeth whenever I entered her room, a lash of fury that stung me through the bond my bite had created. She had made it very clear that I'd ruined her life.

She wasn't wrong.

Which was why I hadn't been up to visit all day. Like a coward, I'd been preoccupying myself with other things.

I sighed deeply then pulled myself away from the call of the night. Johnny and Levi, my devoted mates, were blowing off steam in the sprawling forest outside the mansion, expecting me to join them for a full moon fuc —

The door beside me opened. Lex, Ruby's ever-present guard wolf, stepped outside of the room, pulling my attention out of my completely inappropriate lusty thoughts. I knew my cheeks were ruddy as I turned to greet him.

"How is she?" It was a silly question, considering I could open the threads connecting me to Ruby and feel her mood for myself, but I asked anyway, because I wasn't in the right frame of mind to feel the crushing disappointment and loathing Ruby had for me.

Like I said...coward.

Lex gave me a look that made things as clear as the night sky.

Things are not *good.*

"She's still fighting the shift" — Lex ran his hand over the back of his neck, making it look like he was the one going through a painful transition as he gritted his teeth around his next word — "somehow."

We both knew that Ruby fighting the shift would only lead to bad things.

More pain.

Mental anguish.

Delayed transformation would mean, like tectonic plates shifting, the pressure would build up inside Ruby and the shift would come suddenly, against her will and with devastating consequences.

Broken bones.

Lots of blood.

Death.

Or worse, for Ruby and for all of us, she could turn feral in the most horrific, wild, uncontrollable ways. There was no coming back from that kind of break from reality. She'd give in to every base instinct and would ultimately put the secret world we'd lived in for centuries at risk of exposure. It was a death sentence to her, no matter what.

"Stubborn." Was an understatement when it came to what Ruby was doing. "How does she even have the strength left?" It was a marvel, a true example of what a remarkable human Ruby was, that she was even conscious right now. The fact that she'd spent the last twelve hours punishing herself, working against the change as the full moon crested the clear night sky.

"I think she's running on pure hate right now." Lex laughed as he said that, like his words weren't a slap to my face. "She tried to bite Ari when he suggested she was wasting her time fighting the inevitable, that she should just accept her blessing." Lex rolled his eyes. "Not what she wanted to hear…considering…"

"What idiot told her she wouldn't be able to have kids now, anyway?" I snapped then regretted it immediately. "Sorry." I closed my eyes as Ruby groaned in the next room. "It's not your fault, any of you. *I* did this to her."

"Hey," Lex said as he took me off guard and laid his hands on my shoulders, a gesture that was a huge no-no for any subordinate to an alpha but one that I didn't mind. His lopsided smile was enough to hijack any antiquated werewolf protocols.

Besides, I wasn't the usual kind of alpha.

And I wasn't Lex's alpha. Not yet anyway.

"You saved her life." His smile faded enough to tell me that he believed his own words. "Without your bite, she'd be dead right now. It *is* a blessing."

"She doesn't see it that way." I'd taken the one thing away from Ruby that she's desired more than anything else, a chance to have her own children one day.

Never mind that it hadn't been me who had bitten her the first time. That lovely gift had been from her ex, a man who went after what he thought was a coyote with a pipe only to find out that werewolves didn't back down from humans...*ever.*

Jared's fang scratch to Ruby's thumb, a wound that might have gone unnoticed if I hadn't been paying attention to her discomfort, would have killed her within a day. He'd been too newly formed, too weak to successfully bite another human, but he'd been crazed, confused and had attacked her without realizing what he was doing was irreversible. Ruby wouldn't have made it to the full moon, three days after her initial bite.

According to her, Ruby would have taken death over what was happening to her now. To her, oblivion was a safer choice than becoming one of us. Again, not something I blamed her for. There'd been times in my life that I'd wished I'd never been born a werewolf.

"No one told her, by the way," Lex said, his voice void of all humor, "about the babies."

I should have told her. I should have been the one to explain everything to her. I'd bitten her, stabilized her, she'd woken up and had been coherent. I could have told her.

"Levi explained what would happen to her body," Lex continued.

I held my hand up for him to stop. I knew the rest.

She'd figured it out.

Of course, she had. Ruby was whip smart and cut through the crap better than anyone I'd ever known.

Levi would have told her that her organs were going to die, some she'd expel, which was why transformation was so painful and deadly. Some would shift into something else, organs more powerful and able to handle the demands of a werewolf. Systems would no longer function the way they used to. They'd improve efficiently and handle hormones and chemicals differently. He would have told her that she would become immune to most diseases, that she wouldn't get viruses, that she wouldn't grow cells that were foreign to her body, no cancer...no warts, no *other* things.

She would have known immediately what that meant.

No possibilities of having babies of her own.

"The guys and I were talking," Lex said, plowing through my silence. "We think you need to do your mind meld thing. Make the transition happen."

"Against her wishes." I'd already bitten her without consent. Like Lex said, I'd done it to save her life. I'd gone on instinct and had allowed my beast side to take control, mark Ruby, end her suffering by delivering her to the prison she now found herself in.

A newly turned werewolf. A rare female in a male-dominated world...bitten and barren.

Lex was right, though. No matter how hard Ruby fought, the change would come, with or without her sanity intact. I had the ability to ease her pain and lower her guard enough to let the shift happen.

I closed my eyes, let my shoulders drop, sucked in a deep breath then nodded. I'd already ruined her life beyond repair. Might as well go for a homerun and force her to survive what Jared...what *I*, had done to her.

Lex opened the door to the sounds of agony. Ruby was whimpering, begging without words for someone to put her out of her misery. It sounded like a wounded animal trapped in claws of steel.

I couldn't see her yet, standing just outside her room, but I could feel her despair. It was more than pain. It was heartbreak and grief. She'd lost her life and everything she'd loved. There was no going back to family, to friends. I deserved to know the depths of her anguish.

I shook off my fear, straightened my spine, held my head high like an alpha should, then swept into the room, pulsing calm vibes down the thread that tied Ruby to me and opened myself up to the full force of her pain. It took everything in me to stay on my feet, to endure the anger, sorrow and physical agony of her fight.

As soon as she came into view, I froze, swaying on my feet. Ruby, while still mostly human, looked like a wild thing on all fours, covered in sweat, hair sprouting in ways that looked unnatural and incomplete. Her eyes, now locked on mine, were blazing with werewolf intensity.

Normally warm brown, they shone bronze with a glint that promised reckoning. I didn't need an open thread between us to feel the depth of her fury.

"You!" she growled, spit flying from her lips. "*You* did this to me!" Her words were garbled as fangs got in the way of her tongue.

"Ruby—"

She lurched toward me, swiping her hand like she had claws. Before she could get within reach, she screamed, her neck distorting as it lengthened, her spine popping so loud that we all felt it. A sympathetic groan ran through the room. She fell in a heap, sobbing.

"Make it stop," she begged, clawing at her torso. The fabric of her hospital gown torn where her budding claws had raked. She rolled onto her back, arching through the pain as it racked her.

I didn't have to look at the guys to know what they thought.

I moved to Ruby cautiously, opening the thread that connected us wider so I could ease my essence toward her, giving her peace, sedation for her brain.

She stopped writhing and gouging at her body. Her arms fell limp across her stomach.

"Ruby, it's just going to happen, okay?" I got within her reach, but she didn't lash out again, instead, her eyes dull, she stared, unblinking at the ceiling.

"Let me help you." I lowered myself next to her slowly, like I was working with a wild animal, a wolf in pain. Not that I was afraid she'd hurt me... Whatever she decided to do to my flesh, I deserved it.

I needed some sign of consent.

I wanted to give her a lot of time to stop me. To say no.

I ran my fingers through her hair, brushing what was left of her bangs from her distorted forehead. "Please, Rubes, let me help you through this."

She groaned as another ripple ran through her body, tension making her muscles pop and her veins darken.

A drawn-out minute passed before she curled in on herself as best as she could, rolling to the side, tears running down her cheeks where fur was trying to push out of her pores.

I slipped my other hand under her head and eased her weight onto my lap. She let me hold her like that, and it gave me some comfort. I sent soothing pulses through our link, giving her instant relief so that her gritted teeth were the only lingering sign that another spasm was rocking down her spine.

"I'm sorry, Ruby," I croaked, tears burning the backs of my eyes. "I didn't mean for this to happen."

She shifted her gaze to the side, locking with mine, her shuddering subsiding to small shivers. I pulsed more of my essence, my will, into her. *Be calm, my friend. Let the fight go.*

Her body went limp, but she managed to turn her head so she was staring full on at me.

"I will never forgive you for this, Charlie." She licked her lips, snagging her tongue on her fangs as she did, blood spurting from a new wound, coating her teeth. "*Never.*"

My heart, already in shreds, fell apart for good. "I know, Rubes," I whispered. "I wish it were different."

"I wish I'd never met you," she breathed.

With a body shaking exhale, she transformed, the last of her physical humanity shifting away as she became the wolf she was meant to be—brown fur, so soft to the touch that it set her apart from the males I knew, rippling muscles down her flank, long legs, elegant paws with tuffs of tawny fur between her toes. Her muzzle was sleek, marked by freckles, just like she had as a human, her lashes thick and her whiskers black. She was beautiful…stunning in only the way a female werewolf could be.

My heart swelled and pride cascaded along our bond. She'd done it, come through unscathed.

In one delusional moment, I thought that the physical transformation might have jolted her back to her old self. I wished that was the case, anyway. A future without Ruby's friendship was devastating.

By the way she pushed apart from me — standing on all fours, inches from my face, muzzle down and scrunched, lips up, fangs gleaming and bronze eyes holding the same knowing, the same conviction as before her shift — I knew...

As far as Ruby was concerned, I was her enemy.

Chapter Two

Levi

"I think the best plan is for us to leave." I'd tried consoling Charlie with her favorite, butterscotch cheesecake and plenty of chocolate ice cream, but it was no replacement for a best friend like Ruby.

Charlie looked up at me from her place on the floor, nestled in an assortment of beanbag pillows and heaps of blankets that Johnny had arranged for her. Clever guy had wrapped her up like a burrito, Johnny wedged in along with her like a weighted comforter.

"Run away?" Charlie didn't even sound like herself. Instead, her voice was filled with defeat, disinterest, heartbreak.

I knew she felt guilty for what had happened to Ruby, but I also knew that with time, everyone would adjust to the new reality. Or at least, I hoped cooler heads would prevail so the two friends could find their way back to one another. That was a big hope, I realized, because werewolf heads rarely cooled down enough when there was a grudge hanging between two of them.

Female werewolves were rare, though, and companionship like that invaluable. I knew I'd need to figure out a way for the two to make up if it didn't happen naturally. Charlie may have accepted her life without Ruby if it'd meant Ruby living life on her terms, but this was different. Ruby's life would never be the same, and Charlie felt responsible. I couldn't have my mate so heartbroken that she couldn't live her own life as it was meant to be lived — a queen, a warrior, the love of my life.

"Leave for Italy," Johnny rumbled from his Charlie cocoon. "Mmmm... *Or* we could stay like this forever." He wiggled himself so he was practically on top of her.

I knew from experience that he was probably all kinds of high from Charlie's intoxicating scent. Jealousy was a thick film over my entire body. I hated that Johnny was always able to break down the physical barriers that Charlie sometimes erected. He seemed to be her kryptonite. One little quip and she was butter.

She rolled her eyes.

Or...maybe not.

Charlie sighed, ignored Johnny's bad excuse for flirting, forced him off her, then began to wiggle her way loose from the blankets.

Uh-oh. Not a good sign at all.

"You think it's safe to leave Ruby here so soon after her change?" Charlie strained against the blankets wrapped around her torso, pulling her arms free with a burst of grunts and loosening the blankets around her.

Johnny had sense enough to help Charlie free herself before she got frustrated. She had a quick fuse lately with all the chaos as it had been while Ruby had been fighting her transformation. Even with him shifting and pulling, they were both still stuck.

"I think she'll need time to process everything, come to terms. And I know that Lex, Ari and Rue won't let her out of their sight." I offered a hand, which Charlie took, then heaved her out of the layers, leaving Johnny to wrangle his own way to freedom. "A lot of new werewolves need space. Time to settle."

I set her down close enough for her to lean on me if she wanted.

One point Levi. Zero for Johnny. Nice!

"I'm the last person she wants to see, anyway," Charlie said, her voice hitching a little. "So, you're right. We should keep the plan going."

When she turned into me, I wrapped my arms around her, pulling her closer so she could rest her forehead against my chest. Her arms hung at her sides like dead weight that she didn't have the energy to lift. Johnny glared daggers and I, taking a page out of his bible, winked then flipped him the bird.

"She'll come around eventually, Charlie." I kissed the top of her head, ignoring my brother so I could focus completely on my mate. "You'll see."

"If by eventually you mean in, like, a hundred years, then yeah, maybe." Charlie sniffled, blew out a breath, then swayed away. "Okay, enough wallowing. I can't fix this situation right now, so it's time to go after the big guy."

"I don't have confirmation that Kane's still in Italy, but I've got some associates keeping an eye out," Johnny said as he finally pulled himself from the blankets.

"You seriously know people everywhere, don't you?" Charlie's lips quirked in a sort of smile.

"You betcha, baby!" Johnny winked. "I love Italy…the wine…the pasta…the pastries!"

Charlie and I both rolled our eyes this time.

"This isn't a leisure trip, Johnny," I said. "As soon as we land, maybe even before, Kane will feel the pull to Charlie, which means he'll probably bolt and get as much distance between us and him as possible."

Even without the full story from the scrolls, we had to assume that all our research so far was correct and a third reciprocal bite, bringing Kane and Charlie together, would ignite her stepbrother's final diabolical plans for her. Sal wanted to hunt and kill the most powerful female werewolf in existence, and with Kane's bite and hers in return, that werewolf would be Charlie.

"Kane can't run forever," Charlie said with a swipe of her fingers through her hair. "He's alpha here. He'll need to come back eventually." She brushed lint from her pants. "What's the status of the backdoor deal with the witches?" Even with the slight strain in her voice, Charlie was beginning to sound more like herself. "Are they going to play our game or what?"

"Vince is brokering a deal with some of Sal's castoffs." I hated that we were resorting to working with those little shits, but it was the only way to beat Sal at his own game. Having Vince, Sal's former for-hire accountant and now our double agent, working the details gave me little comfort. The guy was as fucked up as the spell casters. "And yes, they're willing to play…for the right price." Which happened to be a shitload of money.

"Sorry… We're planning on working with witches that Sal didn't want?" Johnny frowned. "What's wrong with these reject spellcasters?"

How my brother could always be a mile behind any active plan was beyond me. It wasn't like we didn't include him in the general information. He had been sitting in the room when we'd come up with the plan. To be fair, I had put a batch of freshly baked tarts on the table, so he'd been stuffing his mouth more than he'd been listening, no doubt.

"Other than being evil and without moral codes?" I noted. "Nothing. They're capable, according to Vince. He's seen them in action. And they know a work-around with the witch text embedded in the contract Kane signed."

We all sucked in a breath at the mention of that contract, the one that sold Charlie to the highest bidder. Thankfully that had been us. The contract itself, with its hidden witch text, was also the source of our impending problems. Sal had used magic to set a trap for Charlie.

"And trustworthy?" Johnny hadn't been part of the actual planning with Vince since there was lingering bad blood between them. "I mean, as far as witches go?"

"They're not loyal like pack brothers," I said. "And sisters…but they like money and they hate Sal, so we're good for now." I'd also been monitoring their adjustments of the contract the times I'd checked in. My abilities to detect casted magic gave me a good idea that the witches were staying true to our agreement. Besides, they wouldn't be getting a full, very generous payment, until I was satisfied. It would be an asset if we had a werewolf with some of the mythical wolf magic that seemed to be mentioned in the parts of the legacy we'd dug up, but I wasn't entirely convinced that those stories were true. I'd certainly never met a werewolf, no matter how old, who could cast complicated spells. My abilities were rare as it was and limited to detection, minor spell work — which I was still figuring out and not very good at — and minimal unraveling of spells. The wolves the old stories talked about were either extinct or had never existed to begin with. The powers that had been described — immobility and containment spells, swaying willpower and altering intentions — seemed more fairy tale than reality.

"So, we go to Italy, find Kane, learn what he figured out about the scrolls, bring him back, complete the trifecta of bites and kill Sal?" Johnny said with a grin. He brushed nonexistent lint from his shoulder. "Piece of cake."

"Sounds so simple when you say it like that," I drawled, heavy on the sarcasm. "I think we need to figure out the logistics of cornering Kane. He's not going to come back willingly and put Charlie in danger."

"If things work the way we've set them up, by the time we get back, the game will have changed." She headed toward the door, Johnny and I staring after her. "Leave Kane to me. I've got a plan. You just need to get me to Italy."

Then she was gone.

"That sounds ominous," Johnny said, his tone all glee. "I love it when she has a plan! Kane is going to be pissed!"

Sibling rivalry didn't stop just because we were werewolves. In fact, it was often worse, especially now that two of us had bonded with Charlie.

Kane was definitely going to be pissed. He thought what he was doing was protecting Charlie. We all knew he was avoiding the inevitable. I'd call him a coward, but there was nothing cowardly about fighting the pull

we all had to Charlie. She was a magnet to our metal —
and a very strong one at that. Kane was fighting against
something unrelenting by keeping himself away. I
didn't envy him one bit for that. I did, however, envy
the look in Charlie's eyes when she talked about going
after him.

I nodded as Johnny tipped his head in my direction
before following Charlie out of the door. We both knew
I'd go along with anything she wanted. Not only was
my heart entwined with hers but she was also my
alpha, and where she went, I went.

Even if it meant facing the wrath of my big brother.

Chapter Three

Charlie

One of the biggest perks about the Duke brother's obscene amount of money was the luxury of traveling to Europe via private jet.

Another perk?

Being sandwiched between two large men in our private cabin with nothing but hours of time to waste.

Levi had my face between his palms, cupping my jaw as he kissed every thought from my head. His firm lips had enough cushion to sink into as he opened himself up, coaxing me to do the same, melting me into a puddle. It wasn't just the bond we now shared or how the mating bite ignited in fissures of heat when my men were close. It was the deep soul level connection, an effervescent pulse that filled me up and made me want to giggle constantly...which was *so* not me.

Johnny was behind me, one arm draped over my waist, teasing the skin along my stomach where my panties offered little barrier to his roaming fingers as he dipped lower, then lower. He kissed along the side of my throat, sending shivers over my scalp and down my spine. I leaned back, urging him to come closer, to meld with me so our skin touched at every point. The press of his hard cock against the curve of my back promised more pleasure was on the way. I just had to be patient, which I never was.

Levi's kiss made me senseless, and when he pulled away, I followed him, trailing his movement to capture his lips again like an addict craving more. I gripped the back of his neck, pulling him to me so I could nip his bottom lip then devour his passion all over again.

Pressed between my men, enveloped in their heat, was more than I could have ever wished for. Their desire consumed me. Their love, pulsing through our bond, filled my heart and made me want to explode like a werewolf-level confetti bomb. Somehow, in all the shit of my life, the death, mistrust, abandonment, I'd found bliss.

The only thing missing now was Kane, my sultry, brooding third.

Just his name in my head had my beast instincts roaring, swallowed almost as suddenly when Johnny slid one hand down my panties, his fingers sweeping along the cleft of my pussy, tormenting with feather touches, making goosebumps rise.

Kane was keeping his distance, but Johnny and Levi were right here ready to give me what I needed.

Johnny hoisted me onto him, my back against his chest, then crossed his other hand over my stomach, caging me to him while he cupped my breast, squeezing gently, stroking reverently. Even with the air conditioner blasting, sweat beaded on our skin, our mingling heat like a furnace, forcing Johnny to flex more in order to keep me from sliding off his chest. He was coordinated enough to angle himself so he could continue kissing down my neck then trailed his tongue up until he latched onto my earlobe. I moaned from deep in my belly, a rumble that sounded more like I was begging than demanding. Johnny laughed, a sound that made me tingle.

Levi tugged at my panties, yanking them down over my thighs then my calves while Johnny adjusted me again, holding me firmly, keeping me from moving an inch, both arms holding me tight while still caressing and stroking, sucking sensitive skin, puckered nipples, driving me wild.

They worked in tandem, no words necessary, both doing what they needed to do to maximize my pleasure. Levi licked his way along my inner thigh, igniting a blaze straight to my pussy and making me rock my hips in a desperate attempt to speed things up. I rolled up to meet his hungry mouth and felt more than heard his answering laugh. Johnny plucked my nipple with his fingers, flicking and pinching while he snaked his other hand down to cup my pussy. Levi's hot breath was right there, like he was waiting for permission. Johnny split his fingers, spreading my folds for his brother's hungry lips.

The moment of contact was pure rapture. Levi pressed against my clit, dipping his tongue low so he could capture the little bud between his lips. He sucked, and I jolted—nerves strung tight, synapses ready to explode.

I writhed, wanting more now, right *now*, chasing an orgasm that I wanted to snatch, but Johnny flexed his arm and pinned me down with sudden force, holding me close so I felt every twitch of his breath and shudder of his body. The scrape of his fangs along my shoulder made me freeze.

Ohhhhh, yessssss.

I wanted his bite again. I wanted to feel his teeth sink into me just as they had when he'd claimed me as his. My own fangs punched through my gums, burning as they slid down quickly to pierce my bottom lip. Blood trickled into my mouth, the copper taste making me moan and buck, despite being caged in Johnny's arms.

The rumble of his laughter and the tease of his fangs along the curve of my neck made my breath catch. Johnny slid his fingers closed, blocking Levi's mouth from my clit before pressing down hard enough to make me cry out.

Barred from my clit, Levi licked his way into my pussy, sucking my lips, delving into my hole, filling me with his tongue, which wasn't near enough girth to satisfy. He was a tease, and I was on the verge of telling him so when his lips replaced Johnny's fingers, taking over where his brother's brutal touch had set me on fire. Levi eased the burn momentarily with his tongue before igniting a raw desire so thunderous that I almost came.

"Not yet, my queen." Johnny's guttural voice rolled through me. It was a stern command, not so unlike Kane's Dom one. "You've got to hold out as long as we do."

He was using a page from his brother's book—one I didn't mind at all. Kane always loved to make me wait, torturing me as I struggled to keep myself from coming without permission.

My thoughts snagged on Kane again…his brooding violence something I desperately missed.

Where are you, Kane? Why aren't you here?

I wanted so badly to have Kane's lips on mine, searing me with his kiss, touching me where his brothers weren't, his cock weeping for the chance to have me. The visual image of three men making me come was enough to send me over the edge.

Pleasure rose swiftly, an orgasm cresting with volcanic intensity so I forgot how to think, stuck on a visual that was all fantasy, lust clouding anything coherent in my brain.

I bucked, the only warning Levi got before I was overcome with a leg-quivering release.

I'd failed to follow their orders.

I wasn't upset about that.

"You're a naughty woman, Charlie," Johnny growled.

Before I could catch my breath or calm my racing heart, the brothers had me flipped and positioned for me to take Johnny's cock into my mouth and Levi's in my pussy.

If this was punishment, I wanted more.

I greedily took Johnny's shaft in my hands, balancing myself with the help of Levi's grip on my hips. Johnny was thick and hard, his head seeping pre-cum, crying for my attention. As Levi nudged me from behind, I braced my knees, opening myself up so he could ram me hard and fast, pushing me forward as I took Johnny's cock deep into my mouth.

My men froze for a millisecond, giving me a chance to adjust to being pinioned on both ends.

My thoughts turned to Kane again, wondering what he would have done to punish me for coming too early. If he were here, my ass would be on fire with his palm print, for sure. He would have tortured me endlessly.

Johnny moved first, once again pulling me from my Kane-riddled thoughts, guiding his cock deeper, nudging against the gate of my throat until I unlocked my jaw, relaxed my muscles and gave him access. I gripped his ass, loving the feel of his muscles as he flexed. He pulled his cock out slowly, for sure torturing himself as his dick glided over my tongue, his head bumping along as I pressed hard to capture its ridge and flick before letting him go.

Levi rolled his hips, drilling me deeply, using his cock to search for my G-spot, while he fingered my clit. He filled me up, stretched me out, made me want to scream for more but only managed to grunt with a dick in my mouth.

With sensations bombarding me, all I could do was ride the waves of pleasure, giving in to the rise with no control of the outcome. There was no fighting this kind of passion, no stopping the pings that flicked against my nerve endings, bringing my body alive so that my skin was almost too sensitive to touch.

Slick with sweat, we fucked one another. Johnny pressed his dick along my teeth, between my fangs in a fit so tight I had a fleeting thought I'd cut him—the taste of his blood a confirmation as it slid over my tongue and riled my beastly needs.

He groaned, one hand in my hair, the other cupping my breast, nipple between his fingers while Levi grunted behind me.

I moaned against Johnny's dick, giving him the vibration, along with the friction. I was lost to these men, never getting enough but still wanting more…and more. Kane should have been here—with us…as one.

Shockwaves rolled through me, a precursor to the explosive pleasure on its heels.

Johnny's thrusts grew urgent, as did Levi's, both men sensing my climax and pumping me harder and faster.

I opened myself to them, my bond to both men alive with pulses that flowed between us…and someone else…a sensation of Kane, his brooding, bossy presence, watching, waiting…dying from need.

The realization that Kane was linked to me, that I'd somehow invited him in so he was straddling my waking world and my unconscious was enough to send me over the edge. My climax exploded, rocking me, along with Levi and Johnny as they pumped me full of cum so it dripped from my chin and my pussy.

Tumbling us all into my dream world where Kane waited.

Chapter Four

You stood fully clothed, your dark-knitted sweater tight across your chest, black army fatigues, which I knew would showcase your mouth-watering ass, steel-toe boots so scuffed that I wondered if you'd gotten into it with some of Italy's werewolves. Your arms were crossed, shoulders back, expression all fury – the 'take no shit' look that could mean an ass smacking for me, which would be welcomed, or a tongue lashing, not the kind I wanted.

Johnny and Levi pulled away from me, disentangling as they realized where we were. Their satiated expressions dissolved as soon as they set eyes on you.

What a buzzkill you were.

While not their alpha, your presence was enough to establish dominance.

"Leave," you ordered, your voice a tumble of gravel.

Given what your brothers had just accomplished, bringing me to climax without you, they smugly complied. I felt the pulse of their reassurance come through our bond, trailing hands, lips, fingers along my still-naked body until they both vanished into the ether, probably about to be fast asleep on the bed next to me.

I pushed myself up onto my knees and faced you, boldly meeting your glare with my own.

"Finally decide to come out of hiding, I see." You'd somehow kept yourself from me in my dreams for the last few days. No matter how hard I'd searched, you were locked away from me. I didn't understand enough about my powers to know how you'd done it, but now that I had you, I wasn't going to let you go. "Where are you?"

"Quiet," you barked as you circled me, making me shiver just from the commanding gesture. I wanted so badly for you to lay your hands on me — to leave marks, to bruise me in the ways you were so good at. I missed the pain you inflicted and the pleasure that followed.

"I told you not to come," you said, but I could tell by the way your eyes danced, sparking molten lava, that you wanted me closer to you, by your side, under your control. You battled your urges, some kind of maniac level of control, ignoring the pull that would bring us together. You wanted me to chase you all over the world, to see how far I'd go. A cat and mouse game. You'd never admit it, though.

I was a wolf, so you knew I'd come hunting. I was a queen in the making, so you knew I'd disobey your commands to stay away.

You closed the space between us, gripping my chin, yanking my face so my neck stretched almost painfully. "You'll put your life in danger, for what?"

There was hurt in your eyes, and that confused me. Why such pain? Was it because you were denying yourself what you so badly wanted?

"For you," I croaked. "For our destiny."

Because I may not have believed the prophecy of your family before, but I did now, in this moment. My need for you suddenly became an unbearable thirst that your presence —

no, your proximity and violent touch — had only made worse. I needed your bite just as you needed mine, no matter the consequences.

"Go home," you growled, but your lips moved closer, a hair's breadth away from mine.

You are the king of mixed messages.

And I knew just how to read you.

I shook my head as best as I could with your fingers digging into my jaw. The lava in your eyes rolled down my body as you took me in. My naked skin was covered in goosebumps, still slick with sweat.

I straightened my spine, forced my chin up, despite your hold on my jaw. I knew what you wanted. I wanted it, too.

"Damn stubborn woman!"

You crushed your mouth onto mine, stabbing my tongue with yours, claiming me as fully as if you were really with me on the plane rather than in my dream world. Your arms were around me, hoisting me against your body, my tender skin still alive with afterglow, delighting in the friction of your clothes, desperate for you to be naked, flesh to flesh with me.

We could get lost in each other just as we had so many times here in the safety of my dreams. We'd melt together, touch all the places that made me moan and made you grunt, writhe, buck.

We could satisfy the nagging itch that wouldn't go away. I raised my hands, ready to thread them in your hair, to climb your body, wrap my legs around your waist.

You pulled away on a gasp, my name garbled, tumbling from your lips. You fought to regain control. You were failing.

You yanked my head to the side, your fingers once again tight on my jaw. I angled up, on tiptoes, ready to have your fangs pierce me deeply.

I knew this was the power of three... I had two bites, yours would be the third, completing the triad, making me the most powerful werewolf queen in the world. We were both compelled to do this. It was nature, instinct. My beastly side howled for completion, but your eyes were warring, reason fighting against instinct.

Even though it wouldn't matter if we bit one another in my dream world, it wouldn't take, not the same as in the real world. Still, the implications would bleed into the reality when we finally caught up with you. You knew, just as I did, that breaching that boundary here, now, in our subconscious minds would mean we'd have less control when we came together again in Italy.

And we would *be coming together in Italy.*

Your groan was brimming with torture.

"We can't. Not yet. Go home," you breathed against my throat, giving me shivers, making my heart flutter. Your fingers lost their grip, and you pushed me away from your body. "The scrolls are gone. The scholars destroyed them. Too scared...too stupid to let history repeat."

This was a shock to me, learning that the elders of our kind had purposefully destroyed the story of my destiny.

I rallied, despite your words. "We know how the story will end." With me as the queen and Sal dead.

"It's too risky. I need more time...more information." But I could tell you didn't believe that. You were scared, too – of letting fate take control, of not knowing how the story would end.

You were also the one who brought me into your clan with the intention of making me queen.

And I was starting to believe you were right.

"Kane," I said, "I'm coming, and there's nothing you can do to stop me."

Chapter Five

Kane

As their flight drew near, I could feel Charlie like a physical pulse in my heart, beating counter to my regular rhythm. It made me jittery, wanting to shift, run, disappear into the mountains — but only if Charlie was at my side.

A dilemma, considering I wanted nothing to do with her.

Not until I could find the truth of our destiny, the truth that the scholars had destroyed in a vain attempt to prevent the rise of the alpha queen.

Anger simmered just below the surface, spiking when Charlie had called me into her head, forcing me to witness her passion and connection with my brothers. Jealousy was a constant bitter reality for me since Charlie had gotten, and given, bites with my brothers, but that wasn't why I'd left Vancouver. I'd needed distance, sure, mostly because I'd wanted to ravish Charlie like an addict seeking a hit and we didn't know enough about what we'd ignite if I had. Sal's contract, his desire to hunt and kill Charlie once she became the powerful werebeast queen she was destined for was one thing…a big thing, yes, but not the only thing. I needed to find the truth…or at least the truth as our species understood it. I wanted to hear it from the scholars. I wanted them to tell me that what we'd started wouldn't end up getting us killed. More importantly, that it wouldn't get Charlie killed.

It had been a foolish underestimation of the scholar's desire to protect historical truth when that truth might mean big change for them. I should have remembered that they only wanted what would maintain their comfortable lives. An alpha queen would, no doubt, stir up a lot of murky shit for them. It would shift control. It might, actually, eliminate the need for the scholars completely. Of course they'd destroyed the scrolls. It probably gave them all heart attacks to know that the alpha queen had been born and was doing what they and the masters had strived to undo… She'd come into her beast.

The scholars couldn't or *wouldn't* give me any assurances that the other outcome depicted in the scrolls they'd destroyed would mean triumph for Charlie. They wanted nothing to do with the possibility of Charlie rising. The scholars, who had intimate knowledge of the scrolls and what they'd prophesied, had been suspiciously silent while I had been there. They were hiding something more than whatever story those scrolls told. It wasn't like I could interrogate them for information or threaten to bash their heads in for it, either. They were revered, protected by guard wolves who would silence me permanently if I so much as looked at the scholars the wrong way. I wasn't scared, but I wasn't stupid, either. At the first no, I'd known what roadblock I faced. The patriarchy was as entrenched here as it was anywhere. Change was evil to them, which made me public enemy number one.

The guards, big, bad, straight-out-of-fairytale-nightmare beasts who bit first, asked questions later, took direction from the scholars. Since the guards had all been bitten by the ancient weres and had multiple bites on each of them, which staggered the loyalty, they were in tune with the scholars' every emotion and whim. I'd been put on notice, a warning when I'd reacted—poorly—to finding out the scrolls I needed had been destroyed. My anger had boiled over, volcanic and messy—which had not been a very good strategy as far as information-gathering went. As a result, I'd been given two hours to get out of town with a pass to spend an indefinite amount of time in the surrounding areas, if only because my reputation for diplomacy had preceded me. The thing was, I got the feeling they'd given me that pass because they were hoping Charlie might show up, which was strange, considering they likely knew who they were dealing with. By destroying those scrolls, they had to know that Charlie would want heads to roll. Even so, it was almost like they'd thrown down the gauntlet, had used the scroll destruction as bait and I'd be damned if I had any part in bringing her here.

So I needed to find out what I could then get the hell out of town...fast.

I planned to figure out if the surrounding area townspeople had any folklore that might prove useful to me. Often, it was the humans who preserved our history through their horror tales and storytelling.

Unbeknownst to them, they were another means of learning about our history, even though it was mixed up in fantasy to some degree and their fear-mongering legends, there were many kernels of truth.

I knew enough of our history to weed through the nonsense.

But, before I could get to that, I had another potential problem. I was being followed by a rogue pack of feral werewolves. Bellagio was a hidden gem in Northern Italy that not only housed the medieval compound where the scholars resided but also many clashing packs and transecting territory lines.

It was surrounded by lush forests and expansive hills and mountains. Beautiful was an understatement, despite its dark and ominous atmosphere. I scented furry things that I ached to hunt rustling in the trees and on the forest floor all around me. It was werewolf paradise and the birthplace of our kind, but it was also rife with competing testosterone. I could practically taste the stuff.

With Charlie on her way to Milan, something the scholars would soon figure out as well, I needed to get the information I could then get the hell out of the area, luring Charlie away in the process. I didn't want a confrontation between her in werebeast mode and the guards protecting the scholars. Not yet anyway. I certainly didn't want her to walk into whatever trap the scholars had set.

I was on a tight timeline in more ways than one.

I needed to deal with the rogue wolves who were trailing me before I could accomplish my research task, though.

I ducked down an alley, keeping my pace steady but not suspicious. There were small shops and restaurants along the cobblestoned roads, but everything was closed. Only a few people were still out and about and not taking advantage of a mid-day *riposo*.

It was quiet. A lazy afternoon. Not ideal for losing a tail.

I ended up weaving down a few more alleys until I found a less-beaten path, a gateway to the forest. As soon as I entered the tree line, I felt the vibration of home seep into my skin and along my nerves, a primordial sense of being in the seat of our kind. I understood instantly why there were so many rogue wolves drawn to this area, why there were territory disputes rumored to happen so often here. It was like Vancouver in its wild and expansive beauty with an extra kick of ancient vibes that piqued my wolf instincts. The scent of wildlife, small furry creatures darting away from me, was a distraction. The dirt and trees, rough bark, rolling stones... They sent tendrils of longing through my body. I wished I could be here for different reasons. I wished I could be here with Charlie so we could explore Bellagio together.

I moved as stealthily as possible without coming off as suspicious. I hadn't passed anyone else on the trail, but I didn't want to seem like I'd picked up on my company, either. If there was going to be a showdown, it needed to happen away from human eyes.

I saw a few trail markers that were meant to guide tourists along the safer routes — unnecessary for someone with a wolf deep within.

Once I'd put enough distance between me and the town proper, I skirted the main trail, weaving around ancient trees, getting a better feel for the uncharted terrain.

I moved stealthily, picking up on the three who were following me coming into the forest, more than fifty paces behind me. Even though I wasn't downwind of them, it wouldn't take much for them to find me here. If I wanted the upper hand, I'd have to get down to all fours and do it the wild way.

A ripple of muscle was all it would take, and I was a split second away from shifting when I heard a thickly accented voice up ahead, a murmur through the leaves that was deep and hearty, a laugh that boomed, bursting with mirth. It, somehow and with no logical reason, eased my anxiety immediately. My muscles unfurled. My movements slowed.

I let curiosity rule and held my shift, moving instead toward the tree line, toward the source of the voice.

"And here he is. The infamous Kane Duke!" Sitting on an ornate metal bench, legs crossed at the ankles, arms out in welcome, was a man with dark hair, olive skin and a thick, but neatly trimmed beard. His eyes sparked dusty green, a wolfly grin on his lips that reminded me of Johnny. "Welcome to Lombardy! You've been exploring the gifts of our mother, I see. The trees, they sing, no?" He held out his hand as he stood, clearly expecting me to shake as he leaned close enough for me to smell cinnamon on his breath. "I'd rather we do this over a drink, wouldn't you?"

I began to reach for his hand but something in his tone made me pause—a familiarity that seemed impossible, his scent now cloying.

"Do what, exactly?" Wariness spiked down my body, bringing me back to myself as I noted the proximity of his scattered pack. The three who'd been trailing me came onto the path and a few more were sculking in the woods. I didn't know what possessed me to lower my guard, but I was cursing myself for getting so caught up in this man.

"You're here for the stories, yes?" He pulled a pack of cigarettes from the back pocket of his cargo shorts, the handshake seemingly forgotten. "The scholars and their guard dogs have kept those damn scrolls under lock and key for centuries, but we" — he thumped his chest, the pack of cigarettes nearly crushed in his hand — "we mavericks, *we* know the truth."

We mavericks... I assumed that was meant to sound like we were on the same side and not like a declaration of war.

"And who are you?" While he seemed to know who I was, I had no clue how or why and who in the fuck he was. I had not even a hint beyond the strange nagging feeling that I'd encountered him somewhere before.

"Me?" He stuck a cigarette in his mouth and one of his pack brothers offered him a light. After taking a deep drag he spoke through the smoke leaking from between his lips. "Lorenzo Lupe, but you can call me Mayor Lore." He blew the rest of the smoke out, squinting at me as he did.

"Lupe?" As in female wolf... It was a long-forbidden surname from a matriarchal line of warriors that I'd come across in some of the history Levi had unearthed — again, relegated to myth and nothing more. There were no Lupe lines in North America from what I'd learned, and I was surprised to hear Lore say the name without so much as a flinch. By all accounts, the surname had been wiped out for centuries, so it almost seemed impossible...

"Damn right!" Lore said with his chest puffed out and that gleam in his eyes again. "I'm all the proof you need that the old girls existed."

"You know why I'm here." It wasn't a question. It was obvious that Lore knew more than I was comfortable with. At the same time, I felt no urgency to get away. This situation was out of my control, and nothing in my body screamed for me to do something about that. I didn't like it, but I also had no desire to change anything. "You're willing to help?"

"Si, *fratello*," he said with a wink. "And I welcome you to my town."

The pack dynamics in Bellagio were volatile at the best of times. Transient wolves would mingle with the local resident packs, form new alliances, stir up shit around the full moon, then move on with new packs — or so I'd heard. It was like the birthplace of our kind invited trouble but something — or someone — made sure Bellagio didn't keep the trouble. I had a feeling I'd just met the man who kept things under control.

I'd missed the full moon by two days, purposely, so right now there was a calm over the town that made this meeting feel a lot more relaxed than it would have a couple of days ago. I was intrigued rather than bothered that Lore seemed to have been expecting me. In fact, every instinct that normally would have been pinging me to be wary was silent.

"Born and raised here, I presume?" Was he self-appointed mayor of the wolves? Not unheard of among highly populated wolf destinations.

"More or less." Lore chuckled. "There are stories about me here, too…just as there are about you, Kane Duke."

"Oh?" Stories I would have heard had I talked to some of the locals? Had he intervened to prevent me from hearing things he didn't want me to hear?

"Don't act so coy... You have her...don't you?" He stuck the cigarette in his mouth then made a gesture of a woman's figure with his hands. "The queen?"

How in the fuck? I somehow managed to keep my surprise from spilling into my expression. "What do you know of a queen?"

He took a drag then handed his cigarette to the guy who lit it. "Me? Oh, I know everything about her." Lore tapped his head and grinned. "And for a small price" — he pinched his fingers together — "I'd be willing to tell you everything I know."

"The scholars say they know —"

"*Merda!*" He gestured around him. "Those old cows think they know it all! They're so out of touch they might as well be in tombs. They've all lost their minds." He moved closer, leaning like he was sharing a secret, the smell of cinnamon strong, invading my senses until I could practically taste it. "Let me make my point clear, *fratello.* I know about Charlotte and the training that happened with the masters. I know how they fucked her up and locked down her beast instincts. I know your legacy and what needs to happen now." He thumped his chest again. "I know *everything* you need to know."

"And for a price, that information is mine?" I wondered what kind of cash he wanted for information I was desperate for. He likely knew enough about me to guess I could pay a ridiculous amount — and I would...for the right information.

Si, my amigo." His grin was disarming. "But later, later, we'll talk of *il denaro*. First, let's get out of this heat. It's time for rest, *reposo*." He waved toward a cobblestoned path behind him. "We'll retire to my place and enjoy vino. Then we'll talk." He rubbed his thumb and fingers, universal sign for money and by the glint in his eyes, a lot of it.

I took one look over my shoulder. His men dispersed, disappearing into the trees so only a soft rustle was left in their wake.

I contemplated for half a second if I was making a mistake following this man.

"Come, brother. You are among friends." Lore's voice boomed in my ears, despite the fact that he'd already started down the path.

I felt an insistent tug to follow and, once again, I let curiosity win. He had what I needed. Somehow, I was sure of it.

Chapter Six

Charlie

We landed in Milan, an hour or so away from where we suspected Kane was.

"You feel that?" A prickling sensation tiptoed over my skin like my fur was rising, ready to burst out. The beast part of me came online, shaking off the satiated high I'd been carrying for most of the trip, thanks to my mates. "Something wicked—"

"This way comes." Johnny rubbed his hands together like a kid hyped to play. "I'm ready for some trouble."

"Easy, brother," Levi said almost under his breath, his teeth clenched and eyes holding a sheen that matched his brother's level of excitement. "We're in their territory now. Let's be considerate guests."

"I'll consider it," Johnny laughed with a wink just for me. "But I've got a lot of energy after that long-ass trip, and I'm ready to use it."

I rolled my eyes but kept moving. The number of times we'd fucked would only have whet his appetite for more of something — violence, it seemed.

Werewolves. Fucking animals!

I laughed to myself. I was feeling a little pent-up, too. I would love to run wild and answer the call of my beast. In fact, I really could also use a steaming, bloody hunk of meat, fresh from the kill, something hearty that I could sink my teeth into.

A raging battle would suffice, too. I could go for ripping the flesh off a worthy opponent, firm up my reputation in Italy, just in case anyone here had any idea about my strength.

The tension that sparked against my instincts came from all around us, so it was impossible to pluck out who might have us in their sights since there were also a shitload of tourists milling about. Hard to zero in on the werewolves among them with so many intermingled scents. And that, expectedly, made it all the more exciting. My hackles were up, and I was with my mates in the desire for a little old-school rumble.

"They'll make themselves known soon enough," Levi said, reading my mood.

Since we didn't know the terrain, we couldn't lead them away from the groups of humans trying to get out of the airport, so our best path was to keep to our plan. "Let's just try not to make a scene here." Which was the exact opposite of what I actually wanted to do.

Just as I said that, a black, sleek stretch limo pulled up in front of us.

So much for blending in.

"Johnny, my brother, welcome to Milan!" A huge and very muscular drop-dead-gorgeous man reeking of werewolf, testosterone and, strangely, pumpkin spice, unfolded himself from the back of the limo, his mouth spread wide in a welcoming smile along with his arms like he was ready to envelop Johnny in a bear hug.

Yep, not subtle at all. Suddenly all eyes were on us, gaping, whispering, aiming phones, thinking, no doubt, that we were celebrities of some sort.

"Robbie, my man! So good to see you again!" Johnny and Robbie did a double cheek kiss while gripping each other's forearms then hugged in that big-man way, with heavy-handed thumps to the back and grunts of familiarity.

It wasn't quite the bear hug I'd expected, but it did stun me that Johnny would let another formidable wolf get so close. Robbie matched Johnny in height, but he was bulkier, a tank of a werewolf. It made me wonder what he looked like as a wolf—broad shouldered, thick legs. He probably tore up the ground as he ran, digging his claws into the earth as well as any opponent who dared take him on. Under different circumstances, I would have loved to see him spar. Hell, I would have loved to battle him myself just to learn what his body could do.

I might have mated with two incredible werewolves, but that didn't stop me from appraising virile males. Robbie was the pinnacle of hunky.

He was wearing a pair of darkly blue jeans that showcased his ass in a snug embrace that only whet my appetite more and a cotton pink shirt that hugged his chest like a second skin, partially unbuttoned to show the ridges of his pecs. These manly men might be a pain in my ass with all the testosterone slinging, but they were very pleasing to the eyes and the overactive erogenous zones in my body.

"I assume this is one of Johnny's *guys* in Italy," I mumbled to Levi who had moved in close to my side as soon as the car had pulled up. I liked the show of possessiveness. It gave me tingles and made me want to drag Levi off to the bushes somewhere.

I locked down my lust and focused on the current situation…somehow.

"You must be Charlie," Robbie said as he pulled apart from Johnny. He moved in to kiss my cheek, but I ducked and weaved as Levi blocked him. No matter how much I liked to look at him, there was no way I'd let him get that close.

"She's not the touchy-feely kind of wolf, brother." Levi held his hand out, letting Robbie know that that was close as he'd get to me.

"Ah, si, si, I got you, man." He shook Levi's hand, pumping it enthusiastically while shifting his wily eyes, a stunning hazel, my way. "My apologies, Alpha Charlotte. I get a little excited to see new faces. And you"—he motioned up and down my body with the same kind of appraisal I'd just given him—"are one of a kind."

"So I've been told." I moved around Levi then held out my hand. "Charlie works."

"Charlie it is." Robbie grinned, gave me a firm shake and a wink. "Pile into my ride and we'll go somewhere more private to talk." He motioned around us with a wave. "We're attracting attention from some undesirables."

"Yeah." Johnny rubbed the back of his neck like he was pushing down his hackles. "We felt them a few minutes ago."

"They won't bother with you while you're with me." He scanned the crowd, his eyes narrowed, lip curled on one side, sending a message to anyone still watching. "I've got a feast ready for you back at my condo and enough security to make any unwanted visitors a moot point." He motioned to the door of the limo. "After you, Charlie."

* * * *

Robbie's condo was located in a cathedral. Nothing too flashy about that…at all.

It was stunning, with gothic architecture, gargoyles at every corner overseeing the premises and above the double metal studded doors that had to be about twenty-feet high and wide enough for the limo to drive right in—which it did, straight to a cobblestoned courtyard that acted as a parking lot. As the big iron doors shut behind us, I understood why security was a non-issue. This location was a fortress.

His place was on the top floor, the penthouse, which meant he had a rooftop terrace that overlooked the city.

I fell in love with the view immediately.

"This is easily one of the most stunning landscapes I've ever seen," I said as Robbie handed me a glass of red wine, house made, according to him. I turned from the mesmerizing cityscape to take Robbie in.

He'd tied his shoulder-length brown curls back, which gave me a clear view of his impressive cheekbones and angled jaw, stubble painted at just the right ration of scruffy to make him look deliciously rogue. His eyes held a similar mischief to Johnny's, which made me relax instantly.

"I'm honored to have you here, Charlie." His voice was soft and deep, like he didn't want the others to hear him. "I've been following your triumphs these last few weeks. You have surpassed all expectation." He had wine on his breath, fruity and sweet. It had tinted his lips a deeper shade of pink. He leaned closer, definitely ignoring the rules of close talk. "I'm in awe."

Forget awe... He sounded lust sick. I'd heard that tone before in my years with my father's cronies, but it'd been a while.

I needed to nip that in the bud. He might be a tasty bit of eye candy, but I wasn't in the market for another mate. Kane was the only one left to bite.

And also, *expectation*? What in the world did that mean?

"Then I'm sure you've heard about the Duke brother prophecy." I kept my voice sweet but firm, easing myself back so there were more than a few inches between our faces. "And I know you can scent the marks I carry."

Robbie narrowed his eyes and pursed his lips, contemplating and questioning. After a few seconds of scrutiny he said, "Never say never, *amore mio*." Robbie grinned, breaking the seriousness of the moment. "There are no limits and no rules for what you can do, *la donna*."

I sipped my wine, enjoying the first hit of robust flavor, briefly entertaining what ifs that I had no intention of pursuing. Imagine a harem of four? Or more? The old Ruby would have cheered me on for such a thought. A jolting pang tore at my mood, reminding me of what I'd left behind. I missed my best friend — especially right now, surrounded by all the manly men and so much temptation.

Hickory-scented smoke wafted toward us, pulling my attention and making my stomach rumble, the only other thing that could shift my mood right now. *Food.*

I scanned the terrace looking for the source, grateful for a distraction. I took in the fig trees, the spread of food on a ten-seat wood table, the fully loaded bar against the back wall and the comfortable looking seating area just behind us.

"What's on the grill?" I nodded to the oversized barbeque, which was being tended to by the werewolf who'd been driving the limo.

"Ribs, legs, T-bone, among other things…an assortment fit for a queen." Robbie was close enough to heat my back.

Johnny and Levi were scoping out the nooks and crannies of the terrace, making sure we were safe. Although a werewolf, in theory, could climb to where we were, Robbie hadn't been lying when he'd said he had security. There were armed werewolves patrolling the building inside and out, checking on us every few minutes by poking their head around corners and giving Robbie a nod.

Seemed like overkill and made me wonder just what kind of dangers were out there waiting for us when we left.

Not that I would have minded a little scrap, along with my unsatiated hunger, I was still itching for some excitement, just not the kind Robbie was hinting at.

I made eye contact with Johnny who winked, then Levi, whose frown was enough to tell me not to lower my guard too much. I pulsed some chill vibes their way, letting them know that I felt in control of things here.

After taking another gulp of wine, I turned back to Robbie, who hadn't stopped ogling me by the feel of his heavy gaze all over my face.

"So you and Johnny…" I said, trailing off to let him fill in the blanks.

"Have known each other for decades." Robbie broke eye contact as he leaned on the wide terrace balcony. "I consider him a brother."

"And you know why we're here?" I cocked an eyebrow at his lascivious grin, marveling at the cockiness of the guy.

"I do." He gulped the rest of his wine then held his glass out to be refilled by a server who'd materialized out of nowhere—a human by the smell of him, a minion by the sheen of his eyes.

"What's your latest information about Kane's whereabouts?" I couldn't help but frown when I recalled Kane's message to me about the destroyed scrolls. It didn't surprise me that the scholars would resort to something so destructive and unhelpful, but it did make me wonder what they were so scared of. "He left the scholars' compound, right?" I thought I'd start with an easy question first, test Robbie's actual knowledge.

"He did, and he indicated that he'd be searching for information via folk tales, which I find brilliant but unnecessary." Robbie pushed himself from the balcony then strolled to one of the plush lounge chairs in the seating area. How he knew Kane's strategy was beyond me…unless he really did have spies everywhere. "He's currently enjoying the hospitality of my cousin who will, no doubt, fill in any and all holes in his knowledge." When I cocked an eyebrow, he continued, "My cousin, Lore, is a collector of the old tales and a connoisseur of the finer things. He's always willing to share the information he gathers."

'For a price' went without saying.

"So you know exactly where Kane is." I was eager to get to him, to see him in person and soak up his essence. It was an ever-present itch, one that I had been pushing deep down, ignoring, distracting myself from for the entire time Kane had been gone. Now that he was closer than ever, I wanted to stop wasting time and get to him finally…before he had a chance to slip away. "You can take me to him."

Robbie's smile faded, and his expression grew dark. "I'd love to escort you there myself but I'm afraid my cousin isn't too pleased with me at the moment." He motioned to Levi, smiling once again. "But your man, Levi, would do just fine heading there with one of my pack brothers as a guide so he can retrieve Kane and bring him here."

Your man. I both loved and hated the sound of that. Levi was no more my property than I was his. "I'll be joining Levi."

"Oh no, Charlie, that wouldn't be wise." Robbie's easy smile crashed into what looked like genuine concern. "The politics here…can be brutal in execution, pack lines and territories in constant dispute." He sounded about as tired of all the bullshit as I was. "The packs circling you at the airport are scouts for some very bad werewolves. They know who you are—word travels fast—and they'd do just about anything to get you for themselves. It would be safer for you to stay here."

"I'm not scared of the wolves here." I held up my hand when he started to argue. "But I'm not stupid, either."

"Please, stay." Robbie's tone had changed, like he had finally realized that I'd be making my own decisions. "Kane will understand the political situation better now that he's meeting with my cousin. He wouldn't want you to go to him, not with things as they are."

"Is he in danger?" It didn't sound like Robbie's cousin, Lore, was someone I'd love to meet, no matter how hospitable he was being with Kane. My hackles tingled, making me want to rub my hand along the back of my neck. I took another sip of wine instead, ignoring the warning for the moment.

"Kane?" Robbie laughed as he waved my concern away. "Not at all. He's considered a god. My cousin is probably fawning all over the man. He has no tact at times, but he's not going to do anything to hurt such a renowned man." He set his glass down on the marble table in front of him. "Kane is under Lore's protection. No harm will come to him. You have my word."

Robbie stood and offered me his hand as Levi and Johnny returned from chatting with some of Robbie's men.

The brothers both nodded the all-clear, and I let the tension bleed from my body when I turned back to Robbie.

He motioned for me to take his arm. "Shall we eat, my queen?"

I glanced at my mates, noted their easy demeanors, despite Robbie's charmer move, then took Robbie's arm, giving him the pleasure of thinking I was falling for his nonsense. He might have been speaking the truth, that Kane was safe and we were, too, but that didn't mean I would be lowering all my defenses.

"Johnny mentioned that, besides looking for Kane, you're also on the hunt for information about your legacy." He led me to the buffet of delicacies.

One of his servers was laying steaming plates of meat down. Warm spices overwhelmed my senses.

My mouth was already watering. My teeth ached to bite into the hearty food. It had been a while since I had my fill of anything. The situation as it was with Ruby, as well as Kane taking off, had killed my appetite. Now that at least one of my problems was close to being solved — getting Kane back in my comfort circle — my hunger was ravenous.

"You know something about that?" Levi handed me a plate, which already had some of my favorites piled on.

I dropped Robbie's arm in favor of food.

"This is the birthplace of our kind, the seat of our history, my friend!" Robbie picked up a rib then stripped it clean, his lips glistening with grease. "I have many stories about the origins of our kind and the matriarchal lineage many of our families, including yours, Charlie, come from."

"The scrolls have given us most of what we need to know, but we're missing the last part, the second pathway of Charlie's destiny," Levi said, sharing more than I thought he would. Not that I had a problem with showing our hand, but it still sat wrong with me that we were relying so heavily on what the scrolls had to say about my life paths.

"Ah, yes, fate and her fickle options. I've heard that the scholars took matters into their own hands. Fearful ancients, bah!" He cut his hand down like he was chopping the air. "They think they're the only ones who know the truth."

"Have you seen the scrolls? Do you know how the story plays out?" I asked, curious about how much Robbie actually knew.

"Me? No." Robbie seated himself at the end of the table where the buffet ended and the dining experience, complete with candles, china and not-pure silverware was set up. "With your permission, I'd like to invite someone here who will have the information you're looking for."

"Who?" Johnny said with a mouthful of food. He was clearly in bliss, his cheeks bulging, but that didn't stop him from blurting more. "Your cousin?"

"Well, yes, actually, but not Lore. This would be my other cousin and Lore's brother." Robbie waved for our wine glasses to be filled. "Our esteemed and undisputed mayor of Lombardy, Alessandro Lupe, who I think you may already know, Charlie."

I blinked at Robbie, sure I'd heard him wrong. Alessandro was someone I did know. He'd been training at the same time I had with the masters, and we'd formed a bond, the kind that happened when two people were in muscle-aching, forever-sweaty, brain-exhausting misery together.

I hadn't seen him since he left the training compound, having graduated in some mysterious way to a different level of hell. I'd missed him, of course, if only because he'd been someone to commiserate with, but I never thought I'd see him again. I hadn't even known his last name.

"If this is the same Alessandro I trained with at the master's compound, then yes, I do know him. I'd love to see him." I frowned, compartmentalizing my unexpected disappointment. *Another delay.* I wanted Kane here more than I wanted to catch up with an old friend. "But we have to find Kane. That's our priority. We don't have time to wait for Sandro once Kane arrives."

"You're in luck then, because Sandro happens to live in this building!"

Chapter Seven

Charlie

Sandro was never meant to be a big tank of a werewolf like the other werewolves I was often surrounded by. He towered over me in my human form at six foot plus, but he was wiry, his muscles ropey and his body lean. It had always given him an advantage with reach when we'd sparred back in the day, but I wasn't without my attributes. Being smaller, quicker and more willing to take him out at the knees had its advantages. He, on the other hand, had always seemed to have some kind of code against playing dirty — or maybe he'd underestimated me like everyone else had.

Not that I wasn't looking forward to seeing him again... It was just...few werewolves surprised me anymore.

Made me wonder how he got himself into the role of mayor. I assumed he'd need to be ruthless to achieve that, so maybe he'd grown up to be more formable than I'd given him credit for. I was cautiously optimistic that if he'd changed, it had been for the better.

"Charlie, you're just as beautiful as I remember!" Sandro held his lanky arms out to me, and, in this case, I didn't hesitate to accept a hug from a long-ago friend. "I've heard you've been kicking some serious ass lately! You've always been a warrior."

Ah yes, the charm... That hadn't changed in the least.

I felt the rumble of his laugh through his chest where I laid my head for the briefest of moments, inhaling the clove musk I remembered from our training days. The intimacy had been earned between us after a year of brutal training at the hands of some of the cruelest teachers.

"Word travels fast, I've learned." I pulled back to get a look at him, appraising how he'd changed physically as he did the same to me.

"You let your hair grow out." I reached up to tug the dirty-blond hunks that fell to his shoulders. "You always kept it cropped so short when we trained."

"You always liked to pull it out in chunks when we sparred. No permanent damage." Sandro laughed again as he ran his fingers through his hair, letting it cascade in silky waves. "It's a look, I guess." Then he smiled his usual goofy smile, his wide mouth lopsided and his dusty green eyes sparkling. "The ladies in Lombardy seem to like it."

I'd been full of pent-up anger and confusion, not much different to lately, when I'd trained with the masters, and, yeah, I'd taken it out on all my sparring partners. If they opened themselves up to an exploitable weakness, I'd use it. I wasn't about to apologize for the way I was back then. It's not exactly an alpha trait to carry guilt or admit to it publicly, but I probably had been unleashing more than I needed to while training with partners like Sandro.

"I bet." I moved back, sensing my mates' discomfort. They weren't insecure men, but they were both vibing we-don't-love-this-guy pulses my way. I didn't have time to explore, but I did want to honor their instincts. "Johnny, Levi, this is Sandro Lupe? Back then, I believe you went by the surname Dario." Which, I'd admit, sounded weird at the time. More like a first name than last.

Sandro didn't address my question, instead moving to shake my mates' hands.

"And the mayor of Milan, I hear," Johnny said good naturedly, like he wasn't sending all kinds of possessive pings my way. "Pleasure to meet you." The men sized each other up as werewolves do, but there wasn't anything beyond the usual testosterone-fueled firm grips and hearty back slaps.

"The mayor of Lombardy, actually," Robbie interjected, stepping next to Sandro. "His territory is far reaching."

"That's an impressive hold on a large swath." Levi shook hands with Sandro next, squinting his eyes in a way that made unease prick a little at my nerves. "I've read that Lombardy is prone to territory disputes, often with so many rogues moving through the province."

Maybe I was misreading Levi's emotional pulses. I wasn't as great at picking up on the nuisances of fluctuating feelings, especially with both men connected to me. Levi's suspicion was perhaps more about something he was sensing from Sandro. *Magic, maybe?*

"I have loyal soldiers who keep things relatively calm, but yes, like most large areas, there are competing interests." Sandro's smile was disarming, and no matter how hard I concentrated, I didn't feel any wariness beyond what my mates were sending me.

Levi was probably being overprotective and a little jealous. All the same, I had to remind myself that I didn't really know Sandro — not anymore, anyway.

"We do our best to keep things civil. There are a lot of humans here, and we rely on them for tourist money. But this is our birthplace, the seat of our kind, so the pull to pilgrimage is strong. There are many wolves who travel here, at times with agendas to stir things up. Nothing serious has happened while I've been mayor, though."

"Is that because you work with witches in some capacity?" Levi lifted his chin, his stance full of tension and the opposite to Sandro's relaxed posture.

Bingo. I knew he'd sniffed out something beyond my range of detection. I forced my expression to neutral, not wanting to set off any alarms for Sandro. No need for him to feel threatened...*yet.*

"I've heard of your talents, Levi. Your predilection for sensing spells is legendary here." Sandro's smile hadn't wavered. It was warm, his expression open. "*La stregoneria,* witchcraft, is rife in Lombardy, with a legacy as long and winding as our own. Even those among us who have very little detection abilities can sense something wicked the moment they come to Milan, where it's most concentrated."

I shared a look with Levi then Johnny, confirming what we all felt at the airport. But here I felt nothing, and I could tell by the way Johnny shrugged that he hadn't either. Levi, our bloodhound for such things, had been on it, as usual. I'd leave it to him to decide if it was worth our worry. I sent a pulse his way to let him know that I trusted his judgment. He nodded in return.

"So, yes, I do work with a select few *strega*. The most powerful, of course, are women." He nodded to me, his face still relaxed. "But there are males — some like you, Levi — with abilities that exceed expectations."

If Levi found it unnerving for Sandro to know about his special kind of werewolf gifts, he didn't let on. I didn't even really understand the extent of Levi's abilities, and I had a feeling that no matter what Sandro thought he knew, it wasn't the entirety.

"You've been studying us." I tried to keep the edge out of my voice. Giving Sandro or any powerful werewolf the benefit of the doubt was difficult. I wasn't surprised to have been thoroughly vetted before we'd even landed in Milan. I would have done the same thing. It did feel like Sandro's knowledge might have gone above and beyond in the research department.

Sandro turned his face to me again, his megawatt smile nearly knocking me back a step.

"As all good leaders would. You and your packs have been stirring a lot of conversations here. Even before you stepped onto the gameboard, Charlie, we've been intrigued by Kane Duke and his brothers. You've built a stronghold that most of your west coast werewolves seem ignorant to." He leaned closer, his voice dropping, along with his smile. "Now that you're connected to the Duke clan, we know change is ripe, and we embrace what may come."

It was a show of allegiance...or at least support. He was standing close enough for me to feel his heat and smell his familiar scent. My body relaxed, no worrisome pulses from Levi or Johnny to stop me from enjoying a reunion with my old friend. An alliance was welcome.

"Robbie mentioned that you would be the one to talk to about maximizing our success." Johnny stepped in, using his body and proximity to force Sandro back from me. "You know information about the legacy—"

"I know things, yes, about Charlie's destiny," Sandro said as he folded his arms then lifted his hand to stroke his stubbly jaw. "I didn't when we were younger, of course, but when the masters split us up—"

"What do you mean, split us up? I thought you'd graduated to the next level." And there it was, another bit of evidence that I'd been ignorant to. I hated feeling off kilter, like everyone else knew the truth of my life, like I was always the last to find out.

Sandro's bitter laugh matched my sudden downshifted mood. "Graduated would be one word for it. No, I'm afraid they didn't like our connection, felt it would only rile up your natural instincts. By then, of course, you'd shown too much potential. They'd consulted the scholars, learned things about your destiny they didn't like, then they acted."

I felt the truth of that like a sledgehammer to my gut. "What did you have to do with that?"

"Me?" He looked at me, all bitterness gone from his eyes. "If we'd stuck together, I believe we would have exploded their comfortable world a decade ago."

My legs wobbled but I locked myself down. "In what way?"

"Your beast, Charlie... It was always just under the surface when we fought. I could see the beauty of your rage, the instincts that were blooming. You were brutal, fierce and so deeply powerful." He moved closer, ignoring Johnny's low grumble. "It was terrifying, intimidating and so damn beautiful. You were on the cusp of something, and the more we worked together, the stronger you got."

"I don't remember." And it hurt my head to even think about my time with Sandro. So much of it was a black hole of nothing. He was there, we'd spent a lot of time together, but my memory of that period of my life, of gaining power as he said, was Swiss cheese...full of holes.

He frowned at the look on my face, pity there and gone in a flash. "They really did a number on you." He clenched his jaw, his eyes flaring. "I regret allowing them to send me away."

"We were kids." I didn't love the unease that crawled over my skin. If I thought I'd had anger issues toward the masters before, I had a feeling it was about to explode. "It wasn't your fault." I felt a pulse from Levi, soothing calm to batter down the shock of this betrayal. Not that I didn't already know that the masters had fucked with me, but this layering of more truths, the calculated way they'd done it... It was maddening. Levi's calm cascaded over the heat of my fury, keeping me from showing vulnerability.

Keeping me in the game.

I cleared my throat and forced a smile. "I'd like to learn more. Anything you know would be helpful. My memories from that time are cloudy." There'd be hell to pay for that, but first I needed to know details.

"They were diabolical in their mind games, those fools." Sandro rubbed his fist into his palm. "They thought they were doing what was best for all our kind but—"

"They were really just looking out for their own damn selves," Johnny said as he touched the small of my back, letting me know he had me, too.

"Right," I said, breathing steadily, controlling my pace to bring my heart rate back to normal.

"As I've learned, though, your destiny was never meant to go that way, anyway." Sandro cocked his head to the side to make eye contact with Levi then with Johnny. "I was never meant to be a catalyst for you. That had to come with time, with these men you've found." He leaned in. "They have been the keys. Your beast side knows this. I sense her rolling beneath your surface, wisdom from centuries of primordial experience there waiting to act. It was never meant to be me." Almost under his breath he added, "Not then, anyway."

I snapped back like he'd slapped me. That was the last thing I needed right now. Another male vying for a place in my harem? *No.*

His laugh was a bark. I'd clearly startled him with my uncontrolled reaction, which made me doubt myself immediately.

"Not like that, Charlie." He patted the top of my head. "I'm merely the wise old man on your journey, here to impart information you need, hoping that you'll extend a kind hand in return and be generous with your grace."

Now he was speaking in the usual code of an alpha male. "What do you want?"

"Only friendship, alliance." He spread his hands out. "A mutual agreement to keep the peace."

I knew there was more to what he was asking. Eventually he'd call on me to pick sides. By then, I hoped, I'd be in a stronger position to call the shots. "That I can do."

"It's settled then. We'll go to my place so I can show you what I've accumulated on your behalf." He looked at Levi. "You, sir, should go to Kane and retrieve him as soon as possible. Lore is delusional and unhinged. While Kane may not be in immediate danger, I can only imagine what nonsense he's filling in his head."

"I'm not leaving Charlie's side." Levi growled, ratcheting the tension all the way up.

Sandro motioned his hands down like that would calm the situation. "I understand the sentiment, but we're old friends. There's no one here she can trust more."

Uh-oh…those were fighting words to my men.

I swung around to face Levi, blocking Sandro from saying more. "What he means, I think, Levi, is that I'll be okay." I stared into his eyes, knowing by the way they sparked, wild blue like lightning. He was fighting back the need to shift to werebeast. That was a card up our collective sleeves that I wasn't ready to share with our present company.

"I'll be fine here." I ebbed reassurance through our bond.

"Your magic detection is an asset on the road, and you'll get to Kane faster without a huge entourage," Robbie said from somewhere behind Levi. "I'll send you with Marco, who knows the fastest way to my cousin's place."

Johnny stepped in beside Levi, and we all exchanged looks. I felt their concern. It bordered on fear, which—I wasn't going to lie—was very unnerving.

While I didn't sense danger from Sandro, we all knew duplicity was rampant among our kind. I sent a reassuring pulse to Levi and Johnny, letting them know that I wasn't about to lower my guard just because Sandro and I had history.

"It's okay, Levi. Go get Kane. We need him here with us." The energy of my words, the feelings that ebbed from me to Levi, was enough to make him relent to my wish. I knew he didn't like it, but he'd do it.

"Don't let her out of your sight, Johnny. I'm serious. There's magic here." Levi kept his voice low as he hugged his brother.

"Got it." Johnny patted his back to punctuate his words.

"Don't worry, Levi. I'll keep Johnny safe." I winked before I slid in between him and Johnny.

I slipped my arms around his waist as Johnny put his on mine, hoisting me between them so he could nuzzle his lips to the back of my neck, and I could latch mine onto Levi's.

If Sandro reacted to this, I didn't know, because in that moment I was lost to my mates, melting with Levi's tongue in my mouth and lips pressed desperately to mine—caged by Johnny's arms, security in their touch.

Whatever our future held, we'd be together, connected by bites and shared blood.

Now all we needed was Kane.

Chapter Eight

Levi

It went without saying that I wasn't cool with leaving Charlie at the cathedral, no matter how long she'd known Sandro for. Even with Johnny there, a fierce protector for sure, I hated having to be the one to retrieve Kane.

And that brought up a whole other storm of issues I was having with my eldest brother, the one who should have known better than to take off on his own to Italy rather than face his issues with Charlie head on.

I'd never say that out loud to anyone, but that's how I was feeling. His my-way-or-the-highway method of dealing with shit was getting on my nerves now that we had Charlie in our lives. Before her, I could ignore him, let him have his way — but now, not so much.

He shouldn't have run. He should have had enough self-control to deal with the magnetism that drew all of us to Charlie. I was stuck fetching his ass when I should have been with my mate, protecting her or, at least, being with her if she needed me to whoop some werewolf ass.

My spell-detecting abilities aside, there was something strange happening at the condo. It was ancient as far as buildings went, sure, which meant it came with imprints of past residents. Priests, nuns, parishioners all pinged at my awareness, roaming the place like they hadn't gotten the memo that they were dead and gone. That was nothing new, no matter where I went. But the weird feeling I had while inside wasn't because of lingering ghosts.

There were spells at play. Some were for protection—that was obvious right off the bat—but there were others I couldn't completely pinpoint, not with the little time I'd spent there. I didn't like what I'd been picking up on, but that didn't mean it was nefarious—just...not right. Or at least, not something I was familiar with—and that made me suspicious. Sure, we were in a different country, different continent even, but most magic vibrated at a certain level. And it was usually something I could see, like auras and swirling patterns, or feel, like a staccato against my nerves. Whatever was going on at the cathedral was different. It just felt off. Not right or wrong, but it made my hackles rise all the same.

Before I hopped onto the stumpy motorbike that Marco directed me to, I cast my own crude spell. I was no witch after all, so my magic casting abilities were limited, but I could at least leave something behind, a little added protection for Charlie and Johnny. No one knew about my magic manipulation. It was too new and too untested, so I hadn't even let my brothers in on my secret. That Sandro had hinted he had information about my abilities had felt like fishing, at best. There was no way he knew that I'd been learning spells and experimenting...or so I hoped. My new skills were untested and therefore unpredictable, so I didn't necessarily want the world knowing about them yet.

I mumbled the last few words of the spiraling spell meant to heighten Charlie's perception of the magic around her and bolster Johnny's awareness in general, as I revved the engine. The least I could do was share my detection abilities with them. Our bond and my link to Charlie had helped strengthen my ability to at least share that part of my skills. It wasn't enough to make me feel comfortable with leaving them behind, but it was something. I knew that, no matter what, we needed Kane with us. If something shitty was going on, a united front was the best course, and Kane, for all his faults, belonged with us.

Marco, a man of few words, nodded a 'go' and we took off, swallowed by the forest as soon as we departed the city.

It took us an hour or so to get to Bellagio where Kane was. We were traveling fast, off the main roads and along a system of dirt bike paths that seemed well worn. I sensed that the paths were a main route for wolf packs, as well as anything on wheels, off the main roads, bypassing speed restrictions and traffic. It took a lot of concentration to keep up with Marco, who seemed perfectly at ease navigating around, over and sometimes through the brush and trees around us. There was a heavy scent of aggression in the woods. My gut said that there'd been lots of turf wars fought here, which left me feeling wary and on edge. Not enough to cloud my innate Kane detection abilities, but that, along with the obstacle course we were on, was enough to distract me so that when we hit the location where my brother was, it came as a bit of a shock.

Marco slowed as we entered the town, skirting the main road that seemed to run down the center of things, and instead taking a side route that brought us onto a steep hill with an almost impenetrable canopy of leaves. The sun broke through like spikes of light, pinpointing exact spots in front of me and making it seem like I was on a quest in a fairy tale.

He stopped at the entrance to a gated compound, and I knew just on instinct that Kane was behind the nine-foot-tall wrought-iron fence.

I expected Marco to push a call button or announce our arrival with a cell phone. What I didn't expect was for him to flip open a panel, type in a code then ease himself back, crab-walking his bike away as the gates opened.

"How do you know the code?" I sensed duplicity immediately but didn't know what direction it was coming from. Clearly Marco was not who he seemed.

Marco grunted but otherwise didn't answer. Instead, he revved his bike then took off through the gates, giving me a 'come or don't' look hastily thrown over his shoulder. I had no choice but to follow.

By the time we reached the main house, which was, in fact, a mansion resembling a stone castle, Kane, along with a group of other werewolves, was standing as if waiting for us.

We killed the engines just as Kane and Marco spoke at the same time.

"Where's Charlie?" Kane growled.

"We have a problem," Marco blurted.

I did a double take. It was the first time I'd heard Marco speak, and what he said was alarming for so many reasons. He'd given no indication on the ride that there was anything to be worried about.

"Would have been nice to know," I mumbled half under my breath. "Charlie is with Sandro, an old friend of hers," I said to Kane, cringing at the sound of those words, knowing my brother would not want to hear that I'd left Charlie with strangers.

Marco nodded in my direction, like I'd said what he was just about to say. "There was little I could do, Mayor Lore." He opened his hands to show defeat.

I snapped my head to take in the man standing next to Kane. Another mayor? Of the same territory? I sensed brotherly discord—and not a quick fistfight then makeup kind.

"Unacceptable," Lore barked. "I asked you to bring her here immediately."

"Someone better tell me what's going on," Kane growled, his body pumped, fists and jaw clenched. He was about to shift to all fours. We both knew he could cover the distance between here and Milan in no time as a wolf.

"Robbie got to her first," Marco said, a little like he was exasperated. "Apparently he and Johnny Duke are like this." He twined his fingers together.

Kane swore under his breath. "What's going on here?"

"Minor setback," Lore said, his voice calm as he made eye contact with Kane. "Charlie isn't in danger."

I frowned at the way Lore's words seemed to affect Kane. My brother, from one moment to the next, went from ramped up and ready to rip some heads off to all tension sliding from his muscles and his face. He trusted this man and took him at his word.

And that was just plain fucking weird.

"I was at the airport waiting, just like you told me to, Mayor, then Robbie pulled up in his limo, all flash as usual." Marco ran his hand through his hair. "I had to fall back so he wouldn't see me there. I got to the cathedral just before they arrived so Robbie wouldn't know I'd been gone."

"I told you—"

"I know, Lore. I know." Marco hung his head, and I could practically feel the shame rolling off him. "Everything happened so fast. But you didn't tell me that Sandro and Charlie had a history."

"I should have. I realize that now." Lore turned to Kane. "My brother, Sandro, was a guest of the masters at the same time that Charlie had been."

"And he's no danger to Charlie?" Kane folded his arms, but not in a 'stand back' kind of way—more like an 'I'm listening' way.

"Danger? No." Lore shook his head, frowning. "But he'll fill her head with nonsense before using dirty magic to achieve his goals."

"Dirty magic?" I knew I'd detected something off, but I hadn't sensed anything like that.

"Love spells. He'll lure her into thinking he's mate potential," Lore said, using his hands to punctuate his words.

"Charlie won't fall for that," Kane said, sounding so sure of himself.

I would have loved to ask him how he knew, since he'd spent so little time with Charlie to begin with. What Lore was saying didn't fit what I'd been feeling back at the cathedral. It wasn't potions that I sensed in the air. It was a vibration that went counter to everything I knew about magic. Lore's explanation made no sense, but the urgency to push him to clarify was slipping away from me with each passing second. I tried to grab onto it, to blurt out questions, to poke holes in what he was saying, but the desire to do that floated away from me.

"He knows she needs three bites." Lore raised his hand when Kane started to speak over him. "He thinks the third bite can be from him."

"You've seen the scrolls?" I said at the same time that Kane asked, "So he wants to bond with her?"

"More than that, he wants to unite our clans," Lore said, his expression hard to read. "And yes, we've seen the scrolls. We were raised by the same mother, heard the same stories that had been passed down through generations of matriarchs. We are direct descendants of the beast queen line." Lore stopped abruptly, rubbing his hand over his face with a sigh. "I'm getting ahead of myself." When he looked at me, then Kane, I knew we were in for a story. "My brother Sandro and I have disputed the reign of Lombardy for the last seven years, ever since he came back from the master's training. They did something to him there, changed him in some way."

"This is what you meant when you told me that Charlie's destiny is tied to yours?" Kane said with a side-eye to me.

The strange vibration I'd felt at the cathedral was back, tickling my awareness enough to shake myself out of the strange complacency I'd slipped into. Whatever had been going on with Sandro was going on here, too. *Magic?* None that I'd ever encountered.

I pulsed my feelers to Charlie, and when she bounced it back with reassurance in the form of love, I doubted my worries. Maybe the brothers had some kind of different aura about them because of their lineage. Maybe Italy was fucking with my mojo. Maybe I'd been overreacting to everything since we got here.

"The scrolls depict two pathways, but there are actually more than that." Lore blew out a breath. "More than you can fathom."

Which made sense. Why would there only be two possible paths to Charlie's ultimate destiny? Nothing was *that* set in stone, not even among our kind.

Definitely overreacting. The tension across my shoulders eased. Not everything we encountered had to be malicious. I'd been edgy since we'd gotten here.

"As I was saying to Kane before you arrived, Levi, like all instances of fate, choice does come into play." Lore echoed my earlier thoughts, pulling me out of my head. "Charlie is on a path that would suggest she take the bite of all three brothers from the Duke clan, but the fact that you're separated from her and that you have no bite marking you, Kane, suggests a deviation."

I shot Kane a hard look. *Of course!* That made perfect sense. Kane had changed the course of Charlie's destiny by taking off, running away like a coward.

"Sandro said he wasn't after Charlie that way," I blurted. He'd patted her on the head like a child.

"You forget, Levi," Lore said. "Power is so very attractive, and my brother will do anything to be close to Charlie's kind of power. He lied."

I had a feeling he wasn't the only one who was lying.

"So, she is in danger?" Kane looked at me with confusion. He was getting muddled, just like I was.

Were we wasting time here? Should we have been riding like hell back to Charlie?

No, she'd indicated that everything was fine. I shook my head at Kane, letting him know that we didn't have to rush back. We could hear Lore out.

"He won't force himself on her, if that's what you mean." Lore snorted. "Not that I think a glorious beast like Charlie would stand for that, anyway. I've heard what she is capable of, what she has already accomplished in Canada." He waved his hand like he was dismissing our worries, and for some reason, it worked. Any budding concern vanished from Kane's face. "With you stepping away from your place by Charlie's side, you've opened the possibilities that anyone could claim the role of the third. Your family isn't the only one with stories of a legacy." He paused long enough for that to sink in. "And I will admit, the path that Sandro is after—the destiny he believes he foresees—could work in making Charlie all-powerful, more so than even the Duke brothers can provide. As I said, we are Lupe. Our ancestors are the very women, the very glorious beasts, that Charlie embodies."

"So Sal's plan may not be a factor at all?" I said more to myself than anyone else. Had we been distracted by the threat of Sal when all we really needed was to empower Charlie with our mutual bites, a triad of bolstering power? It had been the only sure thing we'd known, and now Lore was saying things were more left to chance than we'd thought.

"Sal?" Lore snorted. "The stepbrother? He's a bit player in this game. Yes, Charlie's destiny would change where that is concerned if she decided to move forward with my brother. She would no longer be in danger of Sal's plans. The contract you described, Kane, would be null and void."

I was speechless. Words trapped in my throat. We'd been so short sighted. One look at Kane told me he was thinking the same thing. We'd miscalculated everything.

"It also means Charlie will face other dangers—other werewolves who want to take her down, alpha's who have no interest in losing anything to her." Lore sighed, and it was like he was explaining himself to dummies. "The course she's on with you three? You know how that will end, one way or the other. Any other path leads to the unknown, not necessarily to a bad place for her, though. It could, and likely would, lead to her ultimate success, because she, unlike any of us, is destined to be the highest power."

Chapter Nine

Charlie

Sandro's condo, if possible, was even more extravagant than Robbie's. I was wrong to think that I'd been in the penthouse when it was clear that Sandro, the mayor, held that privilege.

His condo included three floors with twenty-foot ceilings in some rooms and all the rest open to what looked like the original rafters of the cathedral. His grand foyer with black marble and gold flecked floors, spilled into a lounge with leather and wood artisan furniture. The sitting room and dining area would have been where mass once was held. The nave, Sandro called it. Gone were all the pews in rows, although I spotted a few lining the walls, padded with lavender velvet, under the stained-glass windows. The art depicted in the rose windows was vibrantly colored flowers, swirls, nothing left of the religious originals. They splashed vivid colors across the stone floors and made dazzling patterns on the furniture. The kitchen was elevated on the dais where a priest would, long ago, have shared his beliefs and life lessons. Now it was both functional and breathtaking... Levi would have drooled over the counterspace alone. Every modern convenience was present, including a very impressive-looking espresso machine. The stainless steel and glass cabinets and island complemented the old-world charm left behind from the cathedral's past purpose.

The second floor was devoted to bedrooms, one suite generously gifted to me and my mates. It had already been decided that we'd be spending a couple of nights. I was amenable to it, if only because Kane would be arriving sometime soon, I hoped, and we needed privacy to sort shit out.

The third floor was an observatory, but I'd only been given a glimpse before being whisked up another flight of roughly carved stone stairs.

His portion of the cathedral included the bell tower and a multi-tiered terrace, so while he had a similar view to Robbie's on the main patio, Sandro also had levels of perspective to enjoy all the way up to the sky where the bell tower stretched.

We ended the tour there, on the top of the bell tower, with me peering over the stone edge to scan the horizon as the sun settled to the ground, minutes away from disappearing completely. Johnny whistled as he leaned a little too far for comfort over the side.

"You've left the master's compound well behind you, Sandro." I wanted to ask how he managed to accumulate so much wealth. Certainly, a place like this had cost a fortune. But I knew many wolf families had very old money, and Sandro's, likely, was no exception.

It was also possible that he'd usurped whoever had been here before.

"This grandeur is a perk of my standing in the community here. That and a splash of my roots put me in this place. The masters and their ways were a diversion on my path to my ultimate destiny," Sandro said, his chest puffed out, chin raised, "my birthright as mayor of the Lombardy beasts and any who venture into my territory."

It was a stance I'd seen many times in my life from werewolves with soft egos and the desperate desire to prove strength. It hadn't been one I'd expected to witness from Sandro. I glanced at Johnny, who was watching Sandro with a wry smirk. He knew this kind of man too, fragile alphas who had exploitable weaknesses. What it meant was yet to be seen. The Sandro I'd known would never have become one of *those* kind of leaders, but what did I really know about him?

Very little.

It made me wonder who he was trying to prove himself to. Me? My mate? Himself? Was there something more going on here than I was seeing? I stretched my awareness out, giving my beast instincts a chance to suss the situation. What I felt was…well…nothing — or at least nothing that pinged my nerves and made me wary. There was no magic creeping along my skin. No apparent duplicity and yet…something wasn't adding up.

My silence seemed to deflate Sandro's posturing.

"Enough of my vanity." He grinned when I snapped my gaze his way. His skin was deeply olive toned and sun soaked, but I could have sworn there was a ruddy blush to his cheeks that struck me as endearing — a sensation that wasn't expected but that put me at ease. "Sometimes I forget myself and fall into the trappings of mortal men. I've worked very hard to get to where I am, but I don't take it for granted."

This was the Sandro I'd come to know while training with the masters—humble, proud but dedicated to hard work, not one to brag.

"You're eager to get started," he said, his voice softer.

Johnny grunted an obvious duh.

"I've enjoyed the tour very much but, yes, I'd like to see what information you've collected." Because I was here to accomplish two goals... Levi was taking care of the first one and the second one was within reach. I could feel it with unexplainable certainty. Sandro had the answers I needed.

"Follow me, then." Sandro led us back to the observatory where the night sky was visible through crystal clear windows spanning the ceiling in a half sphere.

I had to stop and stare at the breathtaking view. Being this high up, with nothing to get in our way of seeing the night sky, was a gift. It reminded me of nights spent running in the woods, deep in the wilderness, where no city lights faded the splendor of the stars. The waxing moon was a sliver but that didn't matter, because she was right there, seemingly within reach.

"The windows magnify," Sandro said, his voice reverent. "You should see it at full moon."

I had no words, only feelings. I wanted to see it at the full moon. I wanted to experience being washed by her light, bathed in the incandescence that called to my baser instincts. When Johnny came up behind me, I leaned back, taking in the warmth of his body and marveling for a few moments longer at the sight of such beauty.

I could stay here forever. *I want to stay here forever.*

"I think it's best if we start with my line." Sandro's voice boomed across the expansive room, rolling along the ceiling to snap me out of my head.

When I forced myself to tear away from the night sky and from my mate, I saw Sandro motion to a series of portraits on the farthest wall—paintings of women that I hadn't noticed but should have.

They were all clearly alphas, standing regal for the portrait—the artist capturing the glint of power and cunning in their eyes, the proud tilt of their chin, the way their shoulders were rolled back, their brows unfettered by worry and instead broadcasting their confidence.

I followed him to the first one, my body filling with anticipation. My heart thundered, kicking against my ribs. This, I knew, would be enlightening.

"These will, perhaps, give you a picture of my vested interest in your success." Sandro pointed to the first painting.

"Vassa Lupe," I read as I scanned the woman's face. She had sharp, wily blue eyes, the hint of fangs poking her bottom lip, her hair, wild brown curls that rolled over her shoulders and the visible marks of her mates, like tiny starbursts, just beneath the surface of her skin. They were faint, like tiny veins, but I knew what they represented. "Was she"—my beast instincts perked and I choked on the confirmation of what I was seeing—"like me?"

I reached up to run a finger along the many places both Levi and Johnny had marked me. While their bites hadn't left starburst that were visible, I felt them tingle in a pattern that looked exactly like the ones depicted on Vassa.

"She was," Sandro said, eyeing the path of my finger.

His gaze seared me, and I yanked my hand away, suddenly unsure of my standing with him, confused that I gave a damn.

He frowned as he tore his eyes from me, giving his head a shake before nodding to the painting. "Ours is one of many matriarchal lines that existed in centuries old." He pointed to the next portrait, then the next. "These are my ancestors, formidable warriors who carried our line forward, becoming stronger with each generation. Some had the ability to shift into extraordinary beasts. Some had spell-casting capabilities. Some had enough charisma to charm the most stubborn males." As we moved along the wall, I noticed that the paintings became crude, less painstaking and meticulous. "Until they were forced into hiding when the patriarchy took hold, when hunters rose to kill the great warriors and take their power." He paused long enough to run his finger under his eye, as if he were trying to catch a tear before it fell.

The action hit me hard. My throat clogged. Tears burned the backs of my eyes. The helplessness I'd felt when the masters had told me I was a monster came back. The feeling that I needed to hide my true self rose like insecurities. It was like I was experiencing what these warriors had experienced. Beaten down until they felt shame for being different.

Sandro's expression softened. He reached a hand toward my cheek but stopped himself before touching me. "They undermined the females." He spoke like he knew that was what the masters had done to me. "And they used dirty magic, broke covenants. They took what they hadn't earned, what wasn't their birthright to take."

The emotion in his voice, the raw rasp to his words, made my stomach dip in a different way...like he was offering me something. Something I really wanted to take.

"I have no notion of my history." My father only ever talked about these females like they were fairy tales. Or at least, that's how I interpreted his stories. Did I have a legacy like this somewhere in my family tree? "I don't know where I come from." Beyond the obvious legacy of my Larsen heritage, there were so many glaring gaps in my knowledge. Had the masters brainwashed me into forgetting? Did I have all the information somewhere deep in my psyche?

"You don't, yet." Sandro led me to a room off to the side of the main. A library. Not as grand as Levi's back home but impressive in its own right with floor-to-ceiling shelves, all crammed with books and dark wood walls, a coffered ceiling. There was a settee that I wanted to sink into, stretch out on and have my fill of all these books. "I've been researching for you."

My breath caught as we approached the only table in the room.

He'd laid out a series of drawings as if he'd known ahead of time that I'd want to see them. I was either that predictable or Sandro really did know me well enough to anticipate my curiosity—no, my *thirst* for the truth. Some werewolves would scoff at history, preferring to focus on the present and the future. I understood a little better why that was as I let my eyes feast on what lay before me—ancestry lines, fine webs of connection, that went back and back and back. Sandro pointed to the end, where my name was beautifully drawn in calligraphy.

"My family… My mother…" I traced the lines, seeing how my mother's line went back farther than my dad's did. How generation after generation showed the transference of power, the alpha role most recently belonging to men like my Uncle Gareth, back, back to names unfamiliar to me — names my mother had never mentioned beyond stories of my great aunt Sophia, or great-great-grandmother Victoria. Stories that hadn't held as much significance to me then as they did now.

I came from many outstanding women, their powerful DNA infused in mine. A history that had been lost or, for some reason, kept from me.

"Your line was one of the strongest, Charlie." He pointed to the beginning. "Your ancestor was among the first, born directly from the source, just as mine was and a handful of others. The originals, if you will. A cellular anomaly, a trick of witchcraft, some stories say it was a curse. No matter, our kind was born, and it was born with the first female alphas in charge. They ruled, in their version of peace. As you can imagine, werewolves aren't exactly a complacent bunch, but the female warriors were the ones to keep them in line, to uphold the covenants and morals established, to live in unity with humans, along with other creatures of the night. There was diplomacy, but there was also brutality when needed. The alphas at the time were powerful women who bred powerful families, loyal families, bountiful families. Disputes were handled as they needed to be. Territory division was fair and measured, according to merit. They had special gifts to help them rule. Innate abilities. Powers unlike anything you can imagine."

He ran his finger to where the line began to change.

"Until right around here, late in the sixteenth century. They burned witches, and they hunted werewolves. Indoctrination was powerful. The males took advantage of the religious fervor driven by the humans. Things changed."

"The female alphas?" It was hard to swallow that a human misstep had ended it all. Given the powerful legacy that the female warrior wolves had built, for humans to have ignited their demise was unthinkable.

"Tricked. Overwhelmed." Sandro's voice grew straggled. "Lines were killed off. Others went into hiding. Female babies were murdered at birth."

I covered my mouth, a gasp trapped in my throat. My stomach pitched, my anger swelling.

"The stars aligned when you were born." The look he gave me was lacking any bullshit. He meant what he said—not in a romantic way, but in a prophetic one. "Your father, a believer of the old ways, protected you. He did what he could to nurture your innate abilities, to bring out the traits he knew lay dormant in your blood."

"He sent me to the masters." I didn't want to sound petulant, but it was hard to understand why my father would do that if he wanted me to reach my full potential.

"Hindsight." Sandro sighed. "They lied to him, of course. He was betrayed, just as your ancestors were. The fear… It was all the motivation the masters needed to hobble you." He shrugged but not in a dismissive way, more like an it-is-what-it-is way. "You have knowledge that your father didn't."

"Right." Hit with sudden guilt, I winced. My father had done his best. He'd always made sure I was protected. "Why didn't they just kill me?" But I knew why. They were scared enough of Dominic Larsen. They wouldn't dare harm his daughter, not in any visible way. What they had done was far more conniving—warping my nature so that I felt I was an abomination, that my beast was something to be ashamed of.

Sandro talked over my thoughts. "Because they felt it would happen anyway, with time. They knew about the scrolls. They consulted the scholars. They watched the fall and rise of your stepbrother. Sal—"

"He thinks he's going to hunt me down." New anger rose. A beastly rage that made my skin hot. The nerve of Sal to think he would carry on the brutal legacy of the males who'd come before him, to render female werewolves extinct once and for all.

"The masters, the scholars, they think that's the only rightful outcome for you." He tapped the timeline of my ancestors. "They'd do anything to prevent this from happening again."

"That's why the scholars destroyed the scrolls of the alternative ending?" I didn't have a better way to describe my destiny. It seemed like there was no debate in the eyes of the scholars and the masters about how my life should end.

"Their actions can't stop what must happen." Johnny spoke for the first time, his voice firm, committed.

Sandro nodded like they were speaking the same language, even though, for the past few minutes, he'd been acting like Johnny wasn't even in the room with us.

"Do I have a choice in this at all?" Not that I was having second thoughts about taking Kane's bite and giving him mine, not that I was afraid of the plans my stepbrother had for me. But at some point, it would be nice to know I was making these decisions and not being driven to them by the ancient cells in my body.

Johnny held my stare without batting his eyes. We both knew that I'd already made my choice.

"Come on, Charlie. You know this already." Sandro pointed to the lines. "It's in your DNA."

"My legacy." My eyes grew hot, pricking the backs like a torrent was about to explode. I'd never felt like I'd belonged to my clan. I'd never considered myself leadership material. Now…with all this, I felt it in my bones. My destiny was right in front of me. "This must have taken you years to collect." And he'd done it all for my benefit.

My heart swelled in a way I wasn't prepared for. I hadn't given Sandro much thought after he'd left the master's compound, but he'd obviously been thinking of me.

"I did." He turned to me, his expression soft. "I told you when we sparred, I saw what I'd thought was lost. The stories my mother would tell me about the great female warriors, they were myths. She never truly believed, had never dared to hope…and I hadn't either, not until I met you."

"Sandro, I—" I choked on any other words.

"Charlie, this is important to me." He laid his hand on my shoulder. "Our world is focused on the wrong things right now. The ruling class has made it all about fear, anger, shallow egos and fragile leadership."

I couldn't agree more.

"It's time for you to take what rightfully belongs to you — what has always belonged to you."

I swayed toward him. "How?"

"By considering your choices." He cocked an eyebrow. "All of them."

Chapter Ten

Kane

"We have to get back to Charlie." The urgency of this need hammered me. Lore's words had impact. "*The fact that you're separated from her and that you have no bite marking you, Kane, suggests a deviation.*" I should never have left her.

For someone who'd grown up believing in legacies and prophecies, along with the destiny that my mother had insisted was mine, I'd been acting like an idiot.

"We will need to plan accordingly." Lore motioned to a few of his men. "I have no doubt that the second Levi left my brother's place, Sandro initiated his plans."

"Using some kind of magic?" Levi asked. "I detected something but couldn't pinpoint it."

I gave him a look, which he returned just as fiercely. We were treading on unknown territory with Charlie. Yes, she was formidable and could handle herself, especially now that her beast instincts aligned with her human ones. As a promised mate...hell, as a second in command, which I planned to be to her alpha rule, I'd failed miserably. A cohesive unit was needed, not a scattered pack.

"I hesitate to call it magic. It isn't like what you know," Lore said, sharing but also not really sharing what he knew. "When Sandro has a goal in mind, he will go after it using whatever means possible."

Fuck.

Lore swept his hands toward me and Levi. "Come. Let's regroup." When he saw I was about to protest, he added, "We must plan. Rushing in will force Sandro's hand, and he'll take drastic action. Please, trust me on this. I know my brother. Come, sit, eat, drink. My men are gathering what we need."

I'd lacked any sense of urgency, believing, stubbornly, that Charlie would have to come to me if she wanted to talk, and I was furious with myself. I hadn't wanted to admit that I was dying of thirst for a glimpse of her. I hadn't wanted to give in to the ever-constant pull that I'd been feeling since I'd left her in Vancouver. It was a maddening draw, a thundering impulse to find her, bite her, make her mine. I'd separated from her because of my damn ego, and now I didn't want to waste any more time.

All the same, Lore presented a valid argument. We didn't know what or who we were really dealing with, and if Sandro had some kind of special magic, we needed a plan.

We followed Lore into his house, once again entering the lounge area, with white leather couches and gray plush recliners we'd left when Levi had arrived.

The remains of our meal and scattered glasses of wine were no longer present and, in their place, everything had been refreshed. Lore obviously had a quiet army of minions working behind the scenes for the comfort of him and his guests. The same lull I'd felt when we first came into Lore's house cascaded down my spine once again. His place felt like home. Strange, yes, but also very comforting, given that my thoughts swirled around what may or may not be happening in Milan between Charlie and Sandro.

I was in no mood to eat or drink, despite Lore's gestures to take a seat and enjoy. "How could you leave her?" I grumbled over my shoulder at Levi, knowing he was hot on my heels as we entered the room.

"I left her with protection," Levi said with a voice full of doubt.

"With Johnny?" It brought little comfort. "He wouldn't know magic if it hit him in the face." I rubbed the back of my neck, agitated and eager to leave. But not before we heard Lore out and made the right kind of plans.

"No, Kane, I left her with *protection*," he said again, this time making his meaning more obvious.

Wonderful.

Levi had cast some kind of spell, which was something I knew he could, in theory, do. His magic-detecting abilities were unmatched among the werewolves of Vancouver, but his spell-casting was untested at best, reckless and often stemming from emotion rather than a well-thought-out plan. He thought I was unaware of his experiments with spells, and I'd let him carry that false belief, because it hadn't impacted the pack negatively. Now I regretted not putting a leash on his exploration or at least cautioning him more directly. Not that my opinion mattered much to him anymore, because he was Charlie's werewolf, part of her newly formed pack. I had no say any longer in Levi's choices.

Thankfully Lore missed the message Levi was broadcasting, too busy directing staff carrying food laden with desserts to notice us talking, which was good because we didn't need him getting any ideas of Levi's special but untrained skills.

"What is Sandro hoping to achieve with Charlie?" I couldn't keep the aggression out of my tone. I wanted to punch some walls, or, better, Sandro's fucking face. "Is his objective to get her to bite him?"

Which would happen over my dead body.

In other words, never.

"He wants to share in her power." Lore grimaced. "But ultimately, yes. He'll attempt to convince her to go along with his plans." He looked exhausted, ragged, like his brother had tested him far too many times in his life. "He has a delusion about his role in Charlie's life."

"Which means what, exactly?" Levi said, giving me a look that was full of frustration.

Unusual for my brother and really fucking unnerving. It jolted me enough to change my mood.

Now that he was marked by Charlie, Levi must have felt desperate to be with her. Leaving a spell behind to protect her was, no doubt, his way of easing his own impulse to never leave her side. I should have been more considerate of what my actions had done to my brothers, too. Leaving them had been reckless and selfish.

Levi darted his eyes around the room, flitting from me to the food, the staff, then to Lore. He narrowed his eyes, his brow furrowed.

"Our mother would tell us stories when we were pups," Lore began, pulling my attention back to him. He took one of the lounge chairs like a king in his domain, his legs spread as he leaned forward, elbows on his knees. "Tales of strong female warriors."

Sounds familiar. I took a seat on the longer of the two couches, sinking into the baby soft leather that did nothing to ease the vibrating tension in my body. Levi remained standing but chose to lean against the windowsill, no doubt keeping track of what was going on in the courtyard and in the room.

He was on edge. I could see it in the way his shoulders hunched and his jaw flexed.

"Just as yours likely did," Lore said with a nod toward Levi and myself. "Coming from a matriarchal family, too."

His words caught me off guard, but I hid my reaction. Of course, it made perfect sense that we'd descended from the beastly warriors of old. Our mother had never hinted, but for stories like that to exist, to be passed down from generation to generation, there had to be a reason. What Lore was revealing— that the Duke brothers were descended from a matriarchal line—was news to me.

I glanced at Levi, but he was too busy staring out of the window, seemingly lost in thought. Had he known? It was Levi, my nerdy brother, for whom researching was a superpower. He likely had suspected our lineage, but without proof, he wouldn't have said anything, not until he had evidence to back up his claims. The fact that he wasn't reacting to Lore's statement told me enough. This wasn't the first time Levi had heard these words.

"Sandro would scoff at our mother's tales, saying they were myths that made no sense." Lore shook his head. "Mother didn't totally believe what she was saying, either. She would only tell us, she'd always said, because it was in those times that she'd have our undivided attention. She was always trying to find ways to get us to sit still."

Levi pulled his gaze away from the window, acknowledging in his own way, how our mother had used the stories similarly.

"Mother was a defeated female under the law of our father, who was tyrannical. He didn't value the mothers, the women he impregnated. He had a harem that was unmatched and treated those born females as trophies when he was in a good mood and punching bags all the rest of the time."

Our mother had defied the rule of males. She had no alpha. She chose to live wild with us. She had always told us that a moment of freedom was worth more than a lifetime of oppression. It had been harrowing and dangerous, and ultimately it had led to her being hunted by Sal. Not that I blamed her for her own death. She'd lived on her own terms, and I'd always respected her fiercely for that.

"My father sent Sandro to the masters for alpha training," Lore explained. "My brother was one of a half dozen males who were in the running to take over our clan. I, fortunately, was discounted, as I'd never shown enough of whatever it was our father had been looking for to be deemed an acceptable replacement. Our father had selected the choice few, as he'd called them, to be sent for training in different aptitudes. Ultimately, he'd planned to pit Sandro against all the other chosen ones to fight it out for a place in line." Lore sighed. "No one could have known that Sandro would be training with the very female werewolf who was destined to be queen."

"He said that he'd seen potential in Charlie." Levi pushed himself from the window ledge, his undivided attention finally on Lore. "He told her that he'd seen her beast when they were sparring."

"That's what motivated him to take our mother's stories seriously. He suspended his disbelief and embraced it wholly, without question. He would shout it from the mountains if he could." Lore nodded. "According to Sandro, that was when the masters had separated them. I don't know what they did with Charlie." He raised his hand. "I can imagine it wasn't good. But they sequestered my brother, used their own form of torture to attempt to alter his thinking, to make him retract his belief in our mother's stories." Lore spat out a laugh so bitter that I couldn't help but look at Levi with a cocked eyebrow.

Levi only had eyes for Lore and ignored me completely.

"Of course, all that did was make Sandro's conviction stronger," Lore continued.

"Charlie didn't come out of the master training unscathed." Levi's tone was full of heat, but his closed expression made it obvious that he wasn't going to explain how. "The difference was, she had no such convictions. She had been convinced that they were doing what was necessary for her and her family's safety and sanity."

"They are revered for antiquated reasons." Lore's steely eyes met mine. "And there will be a reckoning — but not before Charlie rises."

"One thing at a time for now," I said, despite feeling the opposite. I wanted to hunt those masters down and teach them the meaning of torture. "What happened to your father?"

"What my father hadn't planned for was being killed by one of his overlooked sons, a rogue whose mother he'd cast out." Lore gripped the armrests of his chair, the veins on his hands popping. "Our clan fell apart. Civil unrest and skirmishes broke out nightly. It was bloody. Word got out that my father had died, so every rogue who could make the trip came to the homeland on a quest to take what my father had lost. All my brothers were killed, except for Sandro, of course."

"You became mayor." It didn't sound like Sandro was the type to give up leadership to anyone, let alone a brother who hadn't been chosen in the first place.

"Mayor of where?" Levi blurted with an abrupt laugh. "Sandro said that he's the mayor of Lombardy."

"Yes, well, that isn't exactly what we'd agreed to." Lore got that look of exhaustion again. He slumped into the chair. "It took me decades to regain control... My brother and I had a pact. He would handle the city, Milan, and I would handle the rest. He knew I had a better way with the wanderers, the rogues." Lore looked from me to Levi. "He betrayed me, as I'm sure you've guessed. He felt he was destined for greater things. The years that have passed? In that time, he has made it a mission to accumulate proof of Charlie's destiny and evidence to secure his place in her rise to queen. He'll use whatever means he has to convince her. Not violence"—he raised his hand—"but persuasion in other ways. He's not one to take no for an answer."

"Then he's going to get a rude awakening when he tries that with Charlie." Levi leaned closer to me and whispered roughly, "The feeling I had back at the cathedral is here, too. I don't know what's going on, but it's time to get out of here." He didn't wait for me to respond, and he didn't seem to care that Lore heard his words. He turned then headed right out through the door.

"Whatever your plan is, it needs to happen now." I stood holding my hand out for Lore to take. "And know that if Charlie hasn't dealt with your brother by the time we get there, I certainly will."

Chapter Eleven

Johnny

"Where does your brother come into play here?" I didn't know what was in the air in Italy, but it smelled like a load of bullshit. Or maybe it was jealousy talking, because I didn't love how close Charlie was getting to Sandro, the softness of her voice when she spoke to him...or the way her eyes swam as if she was overcome with emotion.

I wasn't getting a read on her emotions either, which was concerning. It was like, all of a sudden, I was closed off to her. Levi was right to be worried. Something was off here.

I couldn't feel magic like Levi, but I had this bitter taste on my tongue that was anything but normal. It agitated my senses, confused my instincts — but not completely, not enough to make me complacent about whatever was going on.

Sandro blinked slowly, like I'd woken him from a pleasant dream. He frowned in my direction as if he'd forgotten I was there. "My brother has only ever wanted war." His tone was full of vitriol.

Charlie shifted back a step, breaking away from Sandro's immediate vicinity. She shook her head like she needed to physically clear it. Her actions satisfied my uneasy feeling somewhat.

She glanced my way, frowned a what-the-fuck, then turned back to Sandro.

"War with?" Charlie's frown deepened as she scanned the room, no doubt sensing what I was.

A weirdness in the air. Something unsettling. Wicked.

"Anyone, everyone." Sandro waved at us like he's dismissing his own comment, his face contorted with apparent frustration. "He believes our mother's stories, told on her knee when we were pups, which are filled with fantastical untruths. He has no respect for the research I've amassed." He scoffed as he made his way to the other end of the room where a mini bar was recessed into the wall. "He's weak, without a plan, going on what he calls *instinct*." His last word was heavy on the sarcasm.

Charlie shook her head when I made a move in her direction, her hand upturned slightly in a clear stop signal. She scanned the room again, craning her neck, like she was looking for the source of the odd feeling. I did the same, following her path, seeing nothing that would hint at danger.

"I have a very special vintage I'd like to share with you, Charlie." Glasses clinked and the sound echoed toward us like we were under water. Everything slowed, a trail of light moved across my vision as I brought my gaze back to Charlie.

She was waving her hand in front of her face, obviously seeing the same strange trail of color that I was.

"My brother subscribes to the idea that we're meant to be subservient to destiny, that we can't control the outcome of our lives. He claims he's the rightful mayor of Lombardy. The mayor of rogues, perhaps. He thinks he knows all about you, Charlie."

I pulsed a beat of warning to Charlie, unsure if it would actually reach her. There was something blocking me from feeling her through our threads of connection, but perhaps she could still sense me. When she didn't react, I did it again—stronger, longer, putting everything I had into it.

Again, she didn't flinch...too fixated on the movement of her hand as she waved it in front of her face.

I crossed to her quickly, ignoring her earlier silent command to stay put. I tugged her arm, forcing her hand down. She startled, clearly unprepared for my touch. Her eyes, normally a vivid green, were muted, like a film had coated them.

"What the fuck," I growled into her ear, "is happening?"

She didn't look at me. Her eyes were glued to Sandro, staring at his back, narrowed scrutiny. She tilted her head to acknowledge my words. Whatever had happened moments before, the strange fog that had clouded her eyes was gone. The beast prowled just below the surface of her calm.

Sandro turned, holding up a crystal decanter that sloshed with amber liquid. I let my hand drop and forced my face into a neutral expression.

"I hope you like brandy." He held the decanter to the light, letting the crystal shed rainbows over the room. "Such a good year. Over five decades old. I save this for special occasions — for special people, like you, Charlie." The melodic way he said her name. It was hypnotic.

"Water for me." Charlie's voice was clipped, her jaw clenched.

"That's a shame. No, I must insist. Johnny, you, too." Sandro turned back to the bar.

I wanted the decades-old brandy. My mouth watered for it.

"No, thank you." I choked on those words. "Water."

"My heart bleeds." Sandro laughed as he put the decanter down. "You're in Italy." He popped open the cabinet below the mini bar then pulled out a wine bottle. "We don't drink water here. But perhaps brandy is too much for my Canadian friends." He opened a bottle of wine and poured three glasses. "Please, don't insult me. In Italy we drink fine wine. This is my own batch, made with love." He carried the two glasses, his eyes never leaving Charlie's then handed them to us. "Cheers!"

Red and so thick it clung to the glass, the wine looked like poison. I cocked an eyebrow in Charlie's direction when Sandro left to get his own glass from the bar.

Charlie sniffed the liquid, cringed then shook her head.

We both put the glasses down on the table, careful to keep them away from the ancestry timeline.

"Tell me more about your brother, Sandro." Charlie took a few steps in his direction, her body bulking so when he turned, his glassed raised as if to toast, she was towering over him. "The truth."

He took her in, his eyes widening as he saw her transformation—her muscles rippling, fur sprouting, coming into her beast with precise control.

"Charlie…" Sandro's mouth opened. Closed. He lowered his glass. "I've upset you."

"Not yet. But I'm getting there." She opened her mouth and her fangs slipped into place. "I've got a bad taste in my mouth, Sandro," she hissed. "And I can't feel my connection to my mate." She took the glass from his hand then swirled the liquid. "I'm starting to think you've done something to cause that."

"You misunderstand, Charlie." He took a few steps back as she placed the glass next to ours on the table. "I only wanted you to hear me out. To really listen to my proposal."

"A proposal?" She let more of her beast rise, her fur coming in fully, her body growing to its natural size and shape.

"I wanted to wait." Sandro put the table between him and Charlie, as if that would stop her from ripping his head off. "To show you everything I have." He waved his hands over the timeline practically bowing across the table. "My evidence. I wanted to ease you in."

"Ease me into what, exactly?"

"Think, Charlie, about how powerful you'd be if you exchanged bites with the Lupe line."

She backed up a half-step like she'd been slapped. "Motherfuc— You're all the same…power-hungry, conniving…wanting to take—"

"Not like that…n-n-never like that," Sandro stammered his hands up. "I'm not like these brutes you've aligned with."

I growled at the same time Charlie did.

"I would never have bought you as the Duke brothers did." Sandro steepled his hands as if he were praying. "I wouldn't have signed a contract laced with witch text. I would have protected you." His voice rose with each word. "Kane strove to possess you. I propose something altogether different...a mutually beneficial partnership."

I wanted to rip his throat out. Charlie held her hand up, letting me know that she wanted first bite.

"How dare you?" Charlie slapped her hands onto the table. A cracking noise reverberated through the room.

"How dare I?" Sandro laughed bitterly. "Since the moment I first realized...I knew what you were capable of. I knew everyone would want a piece of you, Charlie. I knew I had to find the truth, and it's right here." He jabbed the timeline. "Right in front of you. Here and here." He pointed to splits in the timeline. "Matriarchal lines came together, making more powerful queens."

"And what good did that do in the end?" Charlie spat. "They were still overrun by the lowlife, conniving, power-hungry males."

"Charlie, please listen to me. You're destined to become the most powerful queen there ever was." He pointed to the timeline again as if to strengthen his point. "If you unite our clans, mix our bloodlines, the course of your destiny will alter. The contract with Sal will become null and void. You will rise to your place. It's a strategic move...a wise path."

Charlie hung her head, taking in deep breaths. For a moment, one second of time, my heart clenched so hard at her silence. Would she contemplate it? Would she see his plan as the better one?

The quiver of her body, the way she reined in her anger, it was clear she was trying not to explode.

No, Charlie would never betray us like that.

"You told her you had no interest in her bite." I stepped closer to the table, giving words where Charlie couldn't. "How are you any different from any other werewolves who want a piece of her?"

"I don't have an interest in her." Sandro took me in, scanning me from head to toe. "I'm not attracted to Charlie that way. My proclivities lie elsewhere." He cocked an eyebrow, making his point clear. He didn't want her. He wanted her power. He turned his attention back to Charlie. "The power we could amass, Charlie... You'd be unstoppable."

"And you'd get what?" Charlie lifted her head, eyes bright. "My power? Access to my mates?"

"At least I'm being honest with you. It's more than the Duke brothers did when they bought you, when they took your choice away from you and bound you all to a cruel game of hunt and seek."

Faintly, like a ripple under my skin, I felt a pulse from Charlie, a command to shift. It was like the first gasp of air after nearly drowning. To feel her again was everything.

"You've overstepped, brother." A growl rumbled behind my words. I lifted my face to the ceiling, tilting my head back so I could howl first as a man then, like the flip of a switch, as a beast.

Sandro's gasp was comically loud. I lowered my head to see Charlie shudder. A full body shake, a ripple over her muscles as she gave in to her transformation.

Sandro's mouth gaped as he took in full glory of her werebeast.

"I'm getting pretty sick of men trying to tell me what to do," she growled.

"Charlie, you're even more amazing than I could have ever imagined." Sandro came around the table, rushing to her like he had no sense of self-preservation. "I've done everything for your success. Charlie. I've prepared for this moment. I battled my brother for control over Lombardy. I have the loyalty of a substantial pack. It would all be yours if you unite our families. You've come to me here. Destiny has brought you to Italy...to me. Imagine if I became like this." He pointed at me, his eyes shining, his throat working. "It's more than I could have ever dreamed. I'd triumph over my brother and his misfits. He would bow at my feet. I'd — "

Charlie snatched Sandro up by the throat, cutting off his next words. Rather than fighting her, he fell limp. *Instant obedience. So pathetic.* He closed his eyes, what could only be described as euphoric bliss on his face.

I wanted to laugh, but it would be a bitter thing and might ruin Sandro's moment. The fool thought he was about to get what he wanted. He had no idea what it would mean to be bitten by Charlie in this form.

"You don't know everything about me, Sandro," Charlie whisper-growled. "You don't have a clue what you're asking for."

Pounding on the doors echoed through the building. The calvary had come.

"I think you have company," I said with a nod over my shoulder.

I'd barely turned back when Charlie ripped into Sandro's throat with her beastly fangs and blood sprayed the walls.

Chapter Twelve

Charlie

There was no thought involved in my decision to mark Sandro, infusing him with ownership that instantly made him my underling, along with all the werewolves he'd bitten—which weren't as many as I would have thought.

And something else…a new sensation that I'd never felt before.

It hummed in my veins, like pins and needles but less painful, more invigorating. My beast side soaked it up, unsure what it was but liking it all the same.

Interesting.

I dropped Sandro's limp body to the ground, letting the men who'd come crashing into the room see Sandro's blood dripping from my beastly chin and down my chest. Then, compelled by fury, I tilted my head and roared.

"What have you done?" By the smell of him, the man who spoke was related to Sandro.

His brother no doubt. Sandro's panic surged through our newly formed bond, telling me two things at once. At this moment, he was more scared of his brother than he was of me, and despite his bragging earlier, he wasn't the one in charge here.

This newcomer, sadly, wasn't aware that I was the one in charge now.

I swung my massive body around, ducking as I left the room, noting that the affection I'd felt, the gratitude that had consumed me toward Sandro moments before was gone. It had been a spell, one that Sandro had used to con me — or had tried to, anyway.

The air was heavy with magic, and now that I could sense it clearly, now that whatever shit Sandro had done was cleared from my head, I knew we'd been tricked — betrayed for reasons only these brothers knew. This man in front of me with his sparking eyes was full of danger, power pulsing from him in controlled waves, chaos clearly just under the surface.

The same vibrations of it radiated in my blood and through my body, thanks to my new connection to Sandro.

"What do you want?" I roared at the werewolf who confronted me, spit flying. I was infused with power now that I'd absorbed Sandro's essence, along with the loyalty of his pack.

Now that Sandro's brother was here, brimming with all kinds of 'oh shit' power, the game was just getting started.

Johnny was frozen in place, like a zombie, his arms lank at his sides, his eyes downcast, body swaying.

I tugged at our bond, satisfied when it pulsed vibrantly. He was fine, frustrated by immobility but only incapacitated on the surface.

I did the same with Levi and felt the rushing pulse of urgency bounce back. He was similarly bound, some kind of magic holding him in place just outside of this building. And Kane? I cursed my inability to link to him as easily. If I could slip into my dreamworld, I could bring him in, but that kind of distraction would cost too much right now.

This cocky man standing with no fear in front of me ignored my question. Instead, he stared at his brother...or really, stared at Sandro's feet, which were the only things he could see through the opening to the next room. I'd taken a rather large bite out of Sandro... It would require some amount of healing time for him to regain consciousness. *Oops!*

I licked my lips and bared my teeth when Sandro's brother turned his gaze to me once again.

"You killed him? Your old friend?" He speared me with a look so full of fury that I could appreciate why Sandro was scared. His eyes practically glowed iridescently, a ring of cold fire that was chilling to see. I didn't have to feel it to know whatever power he possessed was more than Sandro had. He was dangerous. "I would have thought better of you, Charlotte."

"He's mine." I moved forward, daring this man to hold his ground, showing him that his magic wasn't going to work on me. "Where is Levi? Kane? What have you done with them?"

If he was shocked that the gigantic beast in front of him could talk, he didn't show it. Instead, his fury melted and in its place was a bewitching grin. He was an opportunist. I could see it shining in his eyes. He actually thought he had control still.

"We're family, Charlie, now that you've marked my brother." He opened his arms like he was expecting me to hug him. "I'm so pleased you agreed to join us. Has he marked you in return? Completed the cycle? Or did I interrupt? I can give you some time alone—"

"It's done." I didn't feel the need to clarify. "Lore?"

His expression was all charm, if you liked a laughing hyena. "I am, indeed. Lore of Lombardy, undisputed mayor and alpha to an international collection of rogues. I've been building a pack for you, Charlie, werewolves on every continent—loyalty that transcends manmade borders and werewolf pack territories. But you should know this by now. Sandro has clearly succeeded in his task, even if it was premature and without my involvement. He's shared our plans with you, yes?"

I let him talk, knowing he was so full of misunderstanding that he'd gloat in his presumed victory. Inside I was reeling. Sandro had wanted my bite, that I knew. But some grand plan for us? No, we hadn't quite gotten that far. I wasn't exactly cursing myself for being impulsive—Sandro got what he had coming—but I would have liked to know his version of this plan. I'd get it later, once he was conscious, but the way his heart fluttered, his fear so palpable that I felt it through the threads that now connected us, I probably should have been more prepared to face Lore, armed with more information.

"You have nothing to be fearful of now." Lore waved his hand toward Johnny. "That being said, I'll keep my spells in place for the time being, seeing that my magic has little effect on you in this form—or, at least, the magic I'm willing to expend right now." He gave me a gross once-over. "You are quite magnificent. A true warrior queen. But you might be more comfortable in your human form. I have a story to tell you that will take some time." His body relaxed, his eyes losing the ring of ice fire that had marked him as dangerous. "Come. Sit with me. Let's hash out the details of our new arrangement."

I contemplated him for a moment, wondering if I should go along with the ruse and humor him or rip his head off now. The impulse was strong, but I really was curious about what the hell was going on.

"*Hear him out.*" Levi whispered to me through our bond. Somehow, he knew what I was debating. "*Buy me some time,*" he added.

This was a new development. "*So we can talk through our bond now?*"

It came naturally, and his voice was as clear as if he was standing right next to me, whispering in my ear.

"*Seems that way.*"

I was more in the mood to damage some appendages, but I sighed deeply, did my best beastly eye roll, then I gave my body permission to shift back to human form. It was difficult, if only because I was craving bloody entrails.

Lore pounced, closing the space between us now that he was significantly taller than me. He circled, even—I could have sworn—sniffed my hair.

Gross.

I let him do his inspection—reluctantly, I might add—giving him a false sense of safety, all the while rankled by his proximity and general audacity.

"You're the one in charge around here?" My words sounded about as tired of the bullshit as I felt.

Lore came around my front, one eyebrow cocked in what I was sure meant he didn't appreciate my tone. "I am." He waved his hands, indicating that the space belonged to him. "You're in *my* domain."

I tried not to laugh in his face. How the egos will fall. These men never learn.

"I thought Sandro was mayor of Lombardy."

"He's the decoy mayor." If possible, Lore seemed even more proud of himself. He puffed his chest out like he was expecting me to stroke him there, like I'd fawn all over him for his clever tricks. "We knew you'd be more likely to trust him than me, although we weren't planning on doing this here." He shot a scathing look at his brother's jutting feet. "I should have remembered my brother's need for attention. I'm sure he couldn't help himself when he had you so close, his goals within reach."

I tried not to take offense that he was talking about me like I was an object…a box to check.

Just kidding, I didn't try at all.

I bared my teeth, the puny human ones and glared at him with an open disdain. He was so caught up in himself that he didn't notice.

He motioned to one of the chairs in the observatory. The moon was high, just a sliver, but still casting shimmer on everything. I sat, willing to comply for now, wondering what Levi was working on to fuck up Lore's shit, wondering how tasty Lore's heart would be when I ripped it from his chest and took a bite.

"You were supposed to be escorted directly to Bellagio, where my compound is and where I have certain contingencies set up." He shrugged as if he didn't care, but the muscles of his neck were so taut, I could practically see them vibrating with tension. "No matter though, it's all worked out."

"Contingencies like spells?" Spells more powerful than what his brother had used? Would they have my bite, no matter what? Consent be damned? Stupid question when it came to werewolves and alphas. There was no such thing as consent.

He laughed, his head thrown back, full belly chortle. He was lucky I didn't throat punch him.

"We're in the homeland, Charlie. It's more than spells. Witch magic can only take you so far." *You silly girl*, his tone said. "We have our own kind of magic here... Don't you feel it?"

"What I feel is" —I swallowed a hot burst of anger, clenched my fists, took a deep cleansing breath, then tried again—"whatever spell Sandro has going here seems to have clouded my ability to detected anything." *Play along and get a prize*. I hated how much it hurt to be as conniving as he was when what I really wanted was guts...spilling all over the marble floor.

"Ah, yes, Sandro does like to dabble. He likely set something up on the spur of the moment when he realized that Robbie had swept you away." Lore shook his head. His cousin, Robbie, was such a nuisance, his body language said. "That boy has betrayed me one too many times but, luckily, my brother got the job done, anyway." Lore sighed. "I'll take care of Robbie before we bond, so that we don't have to worry about his interference. He has this loyalty issue."

Sounded like my kind of guy. "Loyalty to Johnny? One of my mates, you mean?"

"One of your mates." He smirked as he leaned toward me. "Not your second, though. That was supposed to be Kane, but he has failed you, hasn't he?

And you have a need for someone who can take control, guide your pack while you're on the dais, setting tone, looking regal. I'll save you from the dirty work."

The pompous — "I like the dirty work."

"In your beastly magnificence, of course. But we'll need to focus more on the show of it. You'll handle the diplomacy, and you'll allow me to take care of the business of war, wouldn't you say?"

"What war?" Levi's voice was right there, clear as the moon, in my thoughts.

"What war?" I said the words, but in my head I followed up with, *"Levi, darling, I'm about to rip this motherfucker's —"*

"One second." Levi grunted and a flex of emotion shot through our bond. He was clearly getting closer to whatever he was working toward.

"The war your coronation is going to ignite, of course. You're going to topple the biggest, strongest families. I'll make sure of it." Lore took my hand.

If he made any move to kiss it, I was going to blow.

"Like I said, I have international connections. My pack is vast. Once we mate — "

I shook my hand free. "Is this how you're going to woo me? Talking of war, blood, guts?"

"Don't tell me that doesn't appeal." He took my hand again, this time rubbing his thumb along my wrist. "You're made for it, Charlie."

Sadly, it did appeal but not with him at my side.

"My stepbrother's plans…" But I added, *"Levi, come on. Let me end this guy."*

"I'll give you that one bit of fun. A detour. Revenge for the brutality of your stepbrother's existence. I've heard what he did to your mother, to the Dukes' mother. We need werewolves like him erased." Lore pulled me closer, his grip on my wrist tightening. "We'll secure Canada to your satisfaction, but first we must take out the masters and the scholars."

"And erase our history." I dug my heels in, using my calves to leverage me back so he didn't pull me off of the chair and onto his lap.

"The lies, you mean." Lore's patronizing voice was grating.

Buzzing touched my ears, an internal noise that vibrated in my skull and sent shivers over my face. I forced my expression to stay neutral as Levi's voice bounced around in my head.

"He's using some kind of mind control that's unique to his physiology. I can sense it like magic, but unraveling it will take too much time and might have unintended consequences. I don't think I can do much to release us. Sorry, Charlie. I've reached the limit of my abilities."

I smiled to myself. *"No worries, Levi. I've got this."*

The bloody route would solve this problem — which, I'd admit, was always my plan.

Moaning from the next room pulled Lore's attention away. Sandro was waking up. His link to me coming online in a drunken, confused sort of way. The overwhelming smarmy begging and whimpers was a pulse through our thread, pathetic and not something I had time for. I cut him off immediately. Let him simmer in his torment for now.

"While I don't disagree, the masters and the scholars have some explaining to do, I don't think we need to start a war." I wrenched my wrist, pumping up with a little partial shifting then twisting from his grasp.

"How else will we elevate you to the ultimate power position? You're the queen of queens, the one prophesied about. You're here to save our kind, to make us the most powerful—"

"Whoa there, I'm just a woman trying to get some control over her life for once." I coaxed Sandro to get up, a nudge to reveal himself to his brother. "I will admit, your plans sound appealing."

"So humble...and this is why you need me, Charlie." Lore was oblivious to the way my spine snapped straight, to the way my muscles began to bulk. It was a subtle shift, but an observant male would have noticed. "You lack the vision to really put yourself on top. With my coaching—"

Sandro stumbled into the room like he was barely able to carry his own weight, his bloodshot gaze going from Lore then to me. His throat had healed, mostly, and the mark, my mark, on his skin was spreading as my claim took hold.

I stood as Sandro clumsily approached.

"Brother, congratulations on your success. I was just explaining our plans to Charlie—"

Lore's next words froze in his mouth as Sandro dropped to his knees, the thud reverberating through the floor. "My queen." He kissed my feet. "What will you have me do?"

"Sandro?" Lore jumped up, his face red. "Why are you prostrating to your mate?" He looked at me, clearly appalled.

The shiver of transformation quaked through my body as I shifted to my beast. "When I said he was mine," I spoke carefully around my fangs so I was clear, "I meant, I *own* him."

I swiped my clawed hand across Lore's throat, sending a spurting shower of blood all over Sandro. "Just as I will own you."

Chapter Thirteen

Kane

Once we entered Milan, I realized we'd been tricked. It wasn't Sandro who was the threat. It was Lore. From the moment I'd entered his territory — which extended throughout Lombardy, not just in Bellagio like he'd made it seem — I'd been under the influence of something.

The food or drink we'd shared hadn't tasted off or laced with magic. I would have detected that. It was in the essence of his territory, I realized now, and it was a slow burn, like wisps of smoke invading my muscles, my free will. The man had trapped me slowly.

Now, locked in place in his car, seated next to Levi, who was equally as immobile, my need to get to Charlie was near explosive. I was pissed that I'd been duped, only taking a bit of consolation that Levi had been overcome by Lore's brand of magic, too, but not enough to stop the fury from building until I couldn't stand it.

Charlie had been left to handle Lore and Sandro, not that I didn't think she could, but what would Lore's unexplainable power do to her? Would she fall prey like we had? Was she just as frozen in place? Unable to fend off whatever the brothers were aiming for.

Charlie was exceptional in all ways, but whatever Lore was doing to control us was beyond anything I'd ever experienced before. I knew that would be true for Charlie, too. I could only hope that her beastly instincts would kick in and give her an advantage.

I was also pissed that I didn't have the connection to her like Levi did. His bond to Charlie might give him some insight that I couldn't get.

I wanted to fix that immediately.

I wanted to tell her how wrong, how stubborn, I'd been.

I wanted to tear at my skin, gouge the magic from my body that Lore had somehow expertly woven.

But I was stuck, muscles frozen, unable to blink. No matter how hard I pushed, I couldn't even twitch a finger.

I counted on Levi to work some way into Lore's magic and find a mistake he could exploit. Not only was my brother able to detect and cast some spells, but he was also, sometimes, able to unravel them. I truly hoped that was the case right now. The longer I spent like this, trapped in my own body, the hotter my rage flashed. If he didn't get us free soon, I was sure I'd spontaneously combust.

Levi, I prayed, *fix this.*

If there were any weakness in Lore's armor of magic, Levi would find it. He had to.

Just as I thought that, in my peripheral sight, with my eyes burning, I saw Levi's face contort, a grimace that told me everything. He'd found some loose thread and was fighting it, tugging, trying to unravel the spell that bound us…but it wasn't a fast process, and I was impatient. I needed to get to Charlie. I needed to stand by her side while she tore the Lupe brothers to pieces — a small price for what they've done.

Rage continued to bubble through my body, a storm of fury.

I wouldn't leave Charlie to handle this alone. I wouldn't allow a rogue werewolf to overpower me. I was Kane fucking Duke, and I was being denied my mate.

The pull I'd been avoiding, the one that existed between me and Charlie, I'd pushed it deep down into the depths of my soul, but my sudden conviction, my desire to fix what I'd done, caused it to brim to the surface, pummeling me for release. My mate needed me to stand with her. She wanted me there. I didn't need a bond to know that my place was by her side, but I wanted it, all the same. Instead of fighting the pull to her, I let it loose, unleashing the power of desire, wanting and the unstoppable need to follow my destiny and fulfill the prophecy that I'd heard my whole life.

I was to be Charlie's third. I would complete the trifecta. My will and demand to be with Charlie ripped through Lore's hold on me. It burst into my muscles, tearing my body apart with one excruciatingly painful rip until I thought I would explode out of my skin. I roared against the agony, reveling in my sudden freedom, Lore's magical hold falling away, then exploded from the car, taking the door off its hinges in my urgency to get to Charlie.

Everything I felt blurred into a mass of blood and gore as I tore my way through the courtyard and its security, knocking down or taking out any man or wolf that got in between me and my mate.

I didn't need directions. I knew where to find her. I burst through a flimsy wooden door, shattering it to pieces as I stormed up the stone stairs, a back entrance that left little room for my shoulders to squeeze through. I hit one landing, then another, before Marco stepped in my way, blocking the door that was the last barrier to her.

He was a stupid fool if he thought I wouldn't go through him, too.

"Don't come any farther." Marco held a weapon in each hand—curved blades that looked like extensions from his fists, both glowing with something sinister. I knew instinctively that a nick from one of those blades would mean serious problems for me. I'd seen a knife like it, glowing in the limited light, in a display case owned by Charlie's father. He'd called it Wolfsbane, carved from a rare stone that absorbed the moonlight until it was supercharged with iridescent glow... somehow becoming a poison to werewolves.

"Don't do this, man." Marco's voice held no tremors. He actually thought he'd be able to keep me from Charlie. "I'm not going to let you pass, so don't even try."

"You've misplaced your loyalty," I growled. "You're not on the winning team."

"And you've underestimated my alpha." Marco twirled the blades, making them shed rainbows along the walls, dazzling but not lethal.

It was as good a call to action as any.

I dove low, taking him at the waist and drilling him in the kidneys then dodging left so his blades only skimmed my shirt...close but calculated. I spun us both, slamming him into the wall so the plaster cracked and crumbled.

He grunted then drilled me in the side of the head with the end of the blade.

A bomb exploded through my brain, pain propelling me to stomp on his ankle as I leaned into him. I latched onto his wrist, twisting sharply until the bones creaked, then slammed it into the wall, once...twice.

He swung his other arm, but I pushed my shoulders back, pivoting so he couldn't get a good angle to stab me. I pulled his hand away from the wall, gripping a pressure point, knowing his fingers would go numb almost instantly. As he struggled to pull away, I slammed us both back again, pinning his arm against the cracked wall so the back of his hand was wedged into the divot, then punched his forearm.

He yelped and one knife clattered to the floor. I swept my foot, knocking the blade farther away.

He thudded my back, pounding hard with the handle of his remaining weapon, but I used my weight against him, leveraging so his hits were nothing but taps.

He lifted a knee to nail me in the nuts, which I managed to block, but not before he surprised me with a throat punch powerful enough to take away my breath and make my eyes water.

I choked on nothing, no air getting through, trying to keep the panic from setting in as I twisted us around again, using what little momentum I had to flip him around. It wasn't a very powerful body slam, but it was enough to buy me time so I could catch a wisp of breath into my screaming lungs.

I grabbed his throat, wanting to give him a taste of his own medicine when he kneed me once, twice, shattering a rib and pushing what little air I had right out of my body. I bent over double, holding my elbows close, keeping any more hits from damaging my torso. Screaming pain tore along my diaphragm.

I dropped to my knees, hoping the sudden move would throw Marco off balance. I wedged my shoulder into his groin and heaved up, roaring through the agony of shifting rib bones.

Desperation clawed at me. Charlie was close. I would sense her…smell her. She was on the other side of the door. I needed to get to her. I needed Marco to disappear.

A surge of adrenaline burned through me.

I twisted, despite the agony of moving my torso, then wrapped my arms around Marco's waist, ready to use all the power in my legs to move him through the door if I had to.

He raised his arms, no doubt holding the deadly blade dead center to my spine, getting ready to stab me. I closed my eyes, dug my heels in and rammed him against the door with everything I had.

Chapter Fourteen

Charlie

A surge of ravenous hunger walloped me. Kane was coming, moving closer by the second.

I let Lore drop, not caring in the least how hard his body hit the marble floor. He was a loose noodle anyway, all control gone from his limbs. With the way I'd ravaged his throat, it'd be a while before he got up.

As I walked to the door, I shifted to my human form. I was covered in blood — the smell of copper, my perfume, coated in my triumph.

Lore had hundreds of pack members, all clambering for my attention, confused by the sudden change in leadership.

Quiet.

They knew my power. They knew my authority. I silenced them and thrilled at their instant submission. Now things were getting interesting.

"Deal with your brother," I grunted at Sandro, a whip of a command over my shoulder, leaving him to clean up the mess.

There was only one man I needed right now. Even as alpha of thousands, well on my way to becoming queen of beasts, it was Kane I was desperate for. I wanted him to take me, to make me his, to sink his fangs into my skin and claim what belonged to him. Urgency pulsed. Each step I took to the door, a thud of need rippled through me.

Kane was on the other side.

Fighting to get to me.

The door shook with a thunderous bang. Once, twice, Kane was trying to get in, not realizing that the door slid into the wall, a pocket that wouldn't open the way he was expecting.

With partially clawed fingers, I whipped the door open, slamming it so hard into the wall that the frame splintered. The guy fighting Kane held his arms up, clenched in his fists was a blade that reeked of evil and shone of death.

"You'd stab my mate in the back like a coward?" I roared.

Like a viper I struck with my gnarled hand, my partial shift giving me enhanced grip. I snapped him up by the back of his neck with one hand, wrenching him away from his evil attempt to kill Kane. Then, with one mighty shake, I crushed his spine, not caring who he was or what position he'd formally held in Lore's hierarchy. If he survived his injury, he'd be nothing but a bottom feeder going forward. Cowards had no place in my pack.

His body went limp. The only thing holding him up was my tenuous hold on him.

The blade hit the ground and shattered like it was made of glass.

Kane pulled himself up slowly, making eye contact, fire and fury burning back at me. I could see pain written on his face, but I knew nothing would stop him from taking me.

I let the man I was holding drop.

Kane stepped over him, one arm tenderly wrapped around his waist.

"You're hurt," I said, taking a step forward, a hand raised to touch his face.

He straightened himself, hiding a wince as he let his arm down. "Just a scratch."

I cupped his cheek, molding my hand to his jaw, feeling the stubble along his skin, my eyes hungrily taking in his lips before raising my gaze to meet his.

I'd missed him desperately, and now that he was here, right in front of me, need, desire, longing, love all pummeled my heart.

The roar of emotional chaos was reflected back to me in his molten lava eyes.

"Kane." My voice was barely a whisper, words tangled up in my throat. The world fell away from us. No longer caring what happened around me, I tilted my head, exposing the side of my throat so Kane would know there was nothing standing in the way of what we both wanted.

He launched at me, fingers in my hair, yanking my head back, his hot lips consuming me, my body wrapped along his as we twirled into the observatory — bumping into furniture, sliding along the marble.

Kane didn't care that I was covered in another werewolf's blood. I didn't care that his mouth strayed from my lips, nipping along my jaw.

I wanted his bite.

I wanted to be claimed.

Fangs burned my gums, ready to return the action — a bite for a bite, completing the circle.

There was nothing but Kane's hands on my body, his fingers digging deep into my waist, pulling me closer, crushing my breasts to his chest, his heat enveloping me. His scent — clove, musk, forest — tickled my nose. I wanted to devour him…consume him.

We should never have waited. He was mine. I was his. Time was a thief.

The scrape of his fangs along my skin made me shiver.

"Stop!" Levi's voice broke into my consciousness, followed by his actual voice echoing around us. "Stop, Kane! Charlie! Not here. Not yet!"

Hands fumbled at my back, plucking my awareness of things going on outside of our lust. A grip on my shoulder, fingers wedging between my body and Kane's, forced us apart, both of us panting, eyes only for each other, a deep growl exploding from my body. I clawed at whoever was holding me back, digging gorges into flesh.

Johnny had me by the waist, his hold vise tight, even as I ripped his arm to shreds. Through the haze of need, I made out Levi feet away from me, getting farther. He had a hold on Kane, somehow keeping him from charging me again, somehow pulling him away, moving him back until there was enough distance for my mind to clear.

"This isn't the right time," Levi shouted. "You have to wait until we get back home."

Not because we had an audience. Not because they didn't want me and Kane to bond.

I panted through the hunger that clawed at me.

I let rational thought slip in between my desire.

If we bonded now, Sal's plan would take effect in uncharted territory. I had no idea how that would work, but I had a feeling I'd be compelled to head back to Vancouver, putting me at a disadvantage, if only because I'd be under the influence of Sal's spell — or I'd be locked in place here, waiting for Sal to find me. A sitting duck in many ways with no strategic advantage.

And now, somewhere deep inside, a twinge of something different. A wisp of power I'd never tasted before. It surged as I noticed it, like a pet waiting for acknowledgment. I had my own magic, an intuitive knowing of power, courtesy, I realized, of Lore and Sandro. I let a smile play on my face, stunning Levi into silence, probably because I looked deranged.

Infused in me was ancient power…magic that spoke to my beastly instincts. I had become something else entirely, a queen of queens, ability beyond my wildest desires.

I wanted to use it, to weld it against my stepbrother, to put misbehaving werewolves on their knees.

"Charlie?" Levi said, his eyes wary.

Johnny let his arms drop, sensing, no doubt, a change in me, too.

"You're right," I said, brushing my hair back from my face and taking a deep breath. I had new power that would give me an advantage over Sal. I had to bid my time and learn how to use it. But first, I needed to understand the gift I'd taken from Lore and Sandro.

Kane huffed out a deep breath at the same time I did. Levi released his hold. Kane's eyes flashed debate. He was weighing the options.

He narrowed his eyes. A crescendo of anticipation rushed like fire from my scalp to my toes. He launched at me again, taking me up in his arms then heading to the back room where Sandro stood dumbstruck.

Levi and Johnny rushed us.

"I won't bite her!" Kane roared as he spun to face his brothers. "I promise you both, I won't. But I need time with her." He stepped us both through the door. "Alone."

He didn't wait for any further reaction. I pulsed a calm ebb to my mates, letting them know that I had things under control.

At least, I believed I did.

We knew what was at stake.

Kane shoved past Sandro then slid the door closed behind us, shutting us in the room where my collected history lay scattered on the table.

Kane paused long enough to take in the room, then swept us to the settee, placing me there as gently as he could. I tumbled to the side anyway, the momentum of him stepping quickly away causing me to nearly slide right off the chair. I righted myself with a huff, revved up to give him a scathing glare when he barked his first order.

"Take off your clothes." He took several steps back, putting more distance between us when I wanted him to ravage me.

The burning lust shining at me from his eyes, from the way his body shook ever so slightly, from the clench of his jaw and the way his forearms flexed was enough to tell me that he was fighting to maintain control.

This is a bad idea. It was an unwelcome thought, a moment of clarity that I shoved quickly away. I didn't care. I didn't want to deny myself any longer.

Kane steadied himself. He unclenched his muscles, lifted his chin and stared down his nose at me.

Typical Kane.

The epitome of self-control.

We could handle this. He would make sure of it.

He narrowed his eyes and nodded once for me to get on with it.

He was my torture.

He was spicy sugar wrapped around a tangy bite.

He was flame to my wick.

Kane would be mine, that much I knew, but right now he was sinfully forbidden. And he had perfected denial of my wants as effectively as a god before we'd even met in real life. He wouldn't break his promise to his brothers. He wouldn't lose control.

But that didn't mean he wasn't dangerous anyway.

I didn't take my time. I wouldn't dare ignite his wrath, not yet. I stood on shaking legs wanting him to feast on me, his eyes already fire as he watched my clothes drop from my body.

He stalked toward me, making me back up by the ferocity of his heated gaze.

My legs hit the settee and I buckled, letting myself land on my ass, the brocade fabric of the chair a friction that I wasn't expecting but totally loved.

Kane stopped just at my knees, looming over me and staring down.

I bit my bottom lip, gazing at him through my eyelashes, my body hot, desperate for him to touch, to lick, to devour.

He held my chin, caressing where I'd just bitten my lip with the pad of his thumb. He was reverent both in his touch and the way his eyes dove into my soul and stroked my most hidden desires.

I lifted my arms, ready to unzip his pants, my fingers itching to stroke him back.

"Lie down. Spread your legs but keep your feet on the floor." His voice was gruff, strained.

I shivered, dabbed his thumb with my tongue, the offer still there.

"Don't test me, woman!" His command halted my plans for his cock in an instant.

I scooted back a little, pulling away from his touch so I could do as he'd ordered. The settee was firm but comfortable, embracing me like I wanted Kane to. I let my arms drape over my head, my fingers curled along the top, my tits on display, back slightly arched, feet, just by the tiptoes, still touching the floor and legs spread wide.

I was on display, reveling in his gaze as he scanned my body. I wanted to see him sweat. I loved that heat bubbled to the surface of my skin, turning my flesh rosy.

He made a rough noise that sounded pained then paced away from me.

I kept my head down, didn't dare look at his indecision, his inner debate about what to do with me now that he had me where he wanted me. And I couldn't help smirking just a little. I loved that he found me irresistible. His hunger mirrored mine, and the anticipation of how far he would go made my heart thunder and my pussy throb.

I knew the turmoil he had to be feeling because I was feeling it, too. I wanted him to touch me. I wanted him to taste me. But there'd be very little self-control left once that happened.

Would he leave me here? Unsatisfied? I could see how he swayed to the door, the way his broad back stayed turned to me, his shoulders practically hunched.

"Touch yourself." He didn't look at me. He kept himself facing the wall of books. "I want to hear you come."

My body quivered as excitement rolled over me. Understanding dawned.

I'd never had someone witness my own undoing through the sound of my moans.

I kept my eyes closed, my back arched, then snaked my hand down my ribs, along my abs, to my clit.

I let a low hum slip past my lips, not quite a moan but something hungry-sounding, matching the way my pussy pulsed.

He grunted, and I opened my eyes, intent on watching him as he listened to me tease myself. His fists were clenched at his sides, and that alone made goosebumps explode all over my body. My nipples were already hard peaks.

I circled my clit, dancing around the pressure I so badly needed. I could practically feel the blood rush to my pussy, a heavy descent into pleasure that made my head spin.

Maybe if I taunted him enough, he'd stop this game and consume me. Maybe we needed to embrace the risk and do what felt natural.

"Kaaaane." I stretched his name, giving him everything I felt in the desperate tumble of my voice.

Even without him touching me, I felt him in my own fingers, like we were connected through the air. Even without his eyes consuming me, I knew he was aware of every move I made.

I ran my fingers down my slit, teasing my pussy while I touched my nipples lightly with my other hand — one, then the other, circling slowly until the hard little pebbles under the pads of my fingers throbbed.

A little moan slipped out, a whisper meant to torment. He answered with his own tortured sound, like he was melting. His knees buckled enough to let me know he was fighting hard to stay in control.

We shouldn't touch. I sighed from deep into my core. *Coming together is a mistake.*

But his presence in the room was unbearable.

The pulse to possess him, for him to possess me…? It was near painful.

I pushed down on my clit, a moment of pure pain before releasing myself to stroking and rubbing, circling faster. Noise burst from my lips…unguarded, pure animal. I played with my nipples until they ached. I let my head fall back, lost to myself, the sound of my cresting climax slipping from my lips with no hesitation.

I jolted when his tongue touched my inner thigh. My pussy spasmed, my clit on fire.

No. "Yesyesyes!" I shouted.

I cracked my eyes, narrow slits to see Kane's head between my legs, his eyes locking with mine, his lips pressing to my skin again and again.

His touch was electric…incendiary.

My climax peaked and I soared, leaving my body, the room, the universe, while I stared at Kane's amber eyes and knew no matter what, this is what I wanted.

He gripped my legs, opening me wider, my ankles on his shoulders, his hands firmly stroking down, down until he cupped his big hand over my pussy, the heat of his palm making my orgasm vibrate longer, harder, making me shudder as every nerve ending in my body exploded.

I pushed myself up on shaky arms bent at the elbows, daring him to do it, to take what he wanted. The tendrils of my orgasm still rocked through my body.

I licked my lips, a summons, and he locked his eyes there, lust its own expression on his face.

"Charlie," he groaned as he pressed his palm harder, using the heel to rub my already aching clit.

We were so close to having what we both wanted.

"Kane." I let my head drop back, thrusting my chest out, my throat fully exposed. I knew how I looked, what I was offering.

I was temptation…a siren. His undoing.

Chapter Fifteen

Kane

Finally.

It was time.

Consequences be damned. If I took my hand away from her delicious pussy... If I let her scent lock into me, I'd be lost.

She arched her back, her tits on display. I used the other hand to cup one, thumbing her nipple and feeling the jolt of need straight in my cock.

I'd been with Charlie many times in her dreams. I'd been satiated somehow physically, even though we'd never entered the real world any of those times. How I ached for her now was like nothing I'd ever experienced.

I wanted to sink into her, to feel the cushion of her hot, wet hole, trail my tongue over the tender spot on her throat, just under her earlobe, where my brothers hadn't yet marked her. I wanted my fangs to puncture that delicate skin. I wanted her blood to coat my tongue. I wanted to be linked to her so I'd know intimacy like never before.

Staring at her like this, her glistening skin pebbled with goosebumps, her nipples taut, peaked and ready for my lips, her pussy heat radiating into my palm, I was ready. She was ready.

My cock throbbed and my fangs swelled inside my gums, like they were engorged with need and waiting for the command to show themselves.

If we did this... If I let myself have her... If I sunk my dick into her sweet, hot cushion, I'd be lost. It'd be over. My fangs would follow.

I leaned closer, pressed my palm harder against her wet heat. She smelled of temptation, a primal scent that played along my tongue and teased my most primitive awareness. Need, desire surged through my veins, pulsing into my fangs, urging me to get closer.

I pinched, just a little harder, against her nipple.

She moaned that pretty, desperate sound I'd come to crave. She writhed against my touch. She opened her eyes and told me everything with just one hot look.

I could take her. She wanted me to.

Have her completely...just as she would me.

Wet my dick and make her scream my name.

My fangs burned against my gums, tips just poking at the surface. The need to bite unbearable.

There'd be no stopping if I started.

Not with the temptation of everything she was...of everything our future could be.

Consequences be damned.

The pull to be her third mate had been a throbbing pulse in my body from the moment she'd bitten my brothers but now…now, it was too close. A red aura filmed over my eyes. Lust clouded vision.

Make her mine.

Sink my teeth into her.

Taste her blood.

My fangs broke through, dropping suddenly, an explosion in my mouth so my lips parted to accommodate them.

Her eyes widened, not in fear but obvious excitement. She rolled her hips, pressing against my hands.

And I wanted her.

So much.

No thoughts but one.

Mine.

With a roar that came from somewhere deep in my belly, I pressed my head to the back of my hand, took in a steadying breath, inhaling the perfume of what her pussy promised, then ripped myself away.

I was fast, too fast for her to understand with her lust-rattled brain that I was walking away. I was opening the door. I was stepping aside for my brothers. Not easily, no. It took everything in my power not to rip the door from the wall, to punch a hole into the first thing I saw.

I curled my shoulders against her voice as she called out to me.

"Take care of her," I growled to my brothers.

Levi brushed past me, close enough that I could have reached out and strangled him. I held my arms like vise grips against my sides, fighting the impulse to go back into the room to stop Johnny from leaning over her, from taking what I wanted.

She sighed, and it was a mournful sound that crushed my soul. I waited long enough to hear her moan, her tone all different.

I dared to look — to crane my neck enough to watch Levi and Johnny take over where I couldn't. Johnny was between her legs, his face nestled into her sweet pussy.

Levi had his cock in his hand, ready to pierce her lips while he stroked her breasts.

I groaned, the agony of my own willpower like a knife, ripping every vital organ from my body.

She looked past them. Her eyes on fire.

"When the time is right" — my garbled voice caught, tangled up as my fangs began to recede — "*nothing* will stop me."

Chapter Sixteen

Charlie

Holding court atop the cathedral overlooking the Milan skyscape was never something I thought I'd experience, but here I was, sitting like a queen, with my mates at my side and three werewolves kneeling before me.

It was over the top for sure but, Levi insisted, necessary. I wasn't going to lie. The kick of adrenaline at having so much power was intoxicating. For the first time in my life, I felt like I understood my identity and who I was meant to be…a queen.

"The first act of business I think needs to be addressed is relieving you, Lore, and you, Sandro" — I looked at each man in turn, their heads bowed and their gaze on me through eyelashes, scared to make direct eye contact — "of your roles as mayor."

Lore snapped his head up, forgetting himself, his mouth opened as if to argue. I lashed him with a sharp spike through our shared threads, reminding him that I owned his sorry ass now.

"Of course, my queen," Lore mumbled, his face scrunched in obvious pain, as he lowered his head. "As you wish."

"Robbie, you're going to be the mayor of all Lombardy going forward." I hadn't bitten Robbie, but somewhere along the line, either Sandro or Lore had — which was gross if you asked me. Biting family was forbidden in my part of the world. It muddied the freewill that came with being a born werewolf. Not sure how it happened but I couldn't imagine it was a willing thing. All the same, Robbie's loyalty had come with one of theirs, so now he was mine. I trusted him the most out of the three men kneeling before me. With Johnny's endorsement, making him mayor had seemed like the most logical choice.

"I'm honored. Thank you." Robbie kept his eyes downcast. "Your wish is my command." His grin was impossible to hide.

I rolled my eyes. Johnny put his hand on my shoulder and squeezed. There was a belly laugh brewing between the two friends, for sure.

"I expect monthly updates unless something urgent comes up. Now, get off your knees and stop making this weird."

Robbie raised his head. "Your wish is — "

"Enough," I laughed. "You're making it hard to be commanding."

"Sorry, boss." Robbie jumped to his feet. "You have my respect and my loyalty. No joke."

I nodded, then turned my attention to Lore and Sandro.

"You two are going to learn some manners," I said. "But first, I'm going to need you both to fill me in on the power you used to wield." Because, of course, as soon as the chaos settled into something a little less bloody, I'd locked down any magic abilities the two had possessed. I'd give it back if it suited me to do so, but for the time being, they needed a taste of being under someone else's control.

Both men began to talk at the same time.

I dropped my head, exasperated by their unwillingness to be courteous.

With a flick of my mind, I silenced them both sending a zap of pain down the threads that connected us.

Both men moaned and winced.

The silence that followed was bliss.

"Okay, let's try this again. Sandro, tell me what your power entails and how you harness it."

With Sandro, it had been a fog that had clouded my ability to detect the danger I was in.

"My queen, I wanted to first say that I apologize for using my paltry magic on you. It was wrong to deceive you." Sandro's words were rushed, like he was scared I'd zap him again if he said the wrong thing. And he wasn't wrong. I just might. "My power involves clouding judgment and dampening instinct. It allows me, and now you, to cover a space with a film, a way to blur the truth and buy time to achieve your goals."

"Okay, that I know." Well, not exactly but I suspected. "What I want is for you to tell me how I control it."

"I've had all my life to learn, so the only way I can explain is that you need to will it so. You have to be the first to enter a space, otherwise you risk your target feeling the effects come upon them. Then, once you're in position, you walk the perimeter of the space you want to cloud and focus solely on filling it with doubt. It takes concentration but no precision. Just thinking about clouding judgment and creating a barrier to reason is enough for it to start ebbing."

For me to control this power, I was going to have to get very attuned to it. With everything else going on, mastering a new talent was a little overwhelming. I doubted just *willing it so* would work out well for me.

"Anything else?"

"Only that someone with strong enough will power can break free of it...just as you did," Sandro said.

"That's fine." I nodded to Lore. "Speak."

Lore hesitated long enough to tell me he wasn't keen on sharing his secrets.

"I haven't tried it yet, Lore, but I'm fairly certain that I can enter your thoughts and extract the information I want, thanks to our bond." I tugged on the thread connecting us, giving him a mental reminder of my power over him. "I'm not sure what damage that might do, but we could test it."

"That won't be necessary," he said with gritted teeth. "I'll tell you what I know."

"Excellent." I settled back in my chair, looking comfortable when I was anything but. I wanted to get out of this place, to deal with things that needed dealing with then get home to Vancouver. The sooner that happened, the sooner Kane and I could finish what he'd started.

"Like Sandro, my magic comes from our mother's side, which is important for you to know." His eyes were hard as he glared at me. "Something I would have happily shared with you had you—"

I gave him a zap. He crumbled lower, his hands now on the floor holding the rest of his body up.

"I'll do without the lecture." I leaned down. "Tell me what I want to know."

He sucked in a few deep breaths then pushed himself back to his knees. His face was red, blotchy, his eyes bloodshot. I would teach this man some manners myself if he didn't start showing them on his own.

"Your power must have something to do with controlling others' perceptions," Levi said. "You have the ability to keep people calm."

"Yes, or heighten emotions as necessary," Lore said through gritted teeth. "With Kane and Levi, I lulled them into believing that I was trustworthy, that they were safe. I use my voice, touch, eye contact, anything that will establish a physical connection first, which gives me greater control. I'm able to suppress their instincts to be suspicious or to question. I can subdue their need to protect, so self-preservation becomes nonexistent."

"And when you were able to freeze us in place?" Johnny said.

"That takes a little more effort." Lore settled back on his heels, his eyes flashing with determination. "I could teach you, if you'd release your hold on my power. I could show you."

"Ha! Wouldn't that be something," I said. "No, I don't think I'll be doing that any time soon. You're just going to have to explain it to me really well." I tapped my fingers on the arm of the chair. "You're testing my patience, Lore."

"Fine." Lore glowered. "The connection I establish, I use it to layer magic overtop. Like icing, I coat it along the tether I have to my target."

"And you establish this tether with something as simple as eye contact?" Levi said.

"Yes, although touch is the best way, but yes, with practice I was able to enhance my abilities to include eye contact, and even, sometimes, just my voice reaching someone's ears is enough to establish a connection, as long as they're receptive to it." He looked at his brother. "And I don't need to be in a place ahead of time, either. I can command my power at any time on anyone…as your men learned for themselves."

The fool seemed to be bragging. I rolled my eyes toward Johnny, who walloped Lore upside the head.

"Lore" — I pinched the bridge of my nose — "you have one more chance to fill in the gaps before I do something irreversible."

Lore rubbed the side of his head with a glare at Johnny then spoke. "I give the command to stop moving, to pick up the knife…that kind of thing."

He probably really wished I hadn't silenced his powers right about now.

I looked over at Levi, the unspoken understanding passing between us that Lore could have done so much damage if he'd wanted.

"Of course, willpower and overall mind strength can influence how much control I have." Lore nodded at me as I turned my gaze back to him. "You and your men are testament to that. Kane? He was tough to get through, but he wanted so badly to bring information to you. His desperation was palpable." Lore smirked. "And he isn't even your mate."

I stood abruptly, crowding into Lore's space as I bulked up into a semi-beast size. Lore startled, swaying back so he almost fell over his heels.

I shared a brief chuckle with my men.

"I told you everything I know," Lore growled. "The rest you'll have to figure out on your own." He spat. "Without my guidance, it'll be a long road ahead."

"I think I've heard about enough of this." I brushed invisible lint from my jeans then pushed past Lore so he did fall backward this time. "Robbie, your first act as mayor will be to treat these men to a taste of their own medicine. Use your imagination and see where it takes you. You have my full confidence."

Robbie rubbed his hands together. "My pleasure."

I stopped in front of Lore, so close that I forced him to tilt his head back to look at me. "One day, I'll call on you to prove yourself to me. If you don't impress me, I'll make sure you suffer before you die."

Chapter Seventeen

Charlie

The scholar's compound was familiar to me, if only because I'd absorbed enough of the local werewolves to make it so. I didn't have their memories, per se, but I did have a sense of déjà vu about places and people. I, also very carefully, let their emotions slip through my barriers just enough to give an impression.

Scholar's compound...bad.

Not bad as in dangerous — more like bad as in elitist, lying scum. Either way, I was ready for whatever might come.

The guard wolves who answered to the scholars were definitely big and bad and totally dangerous, but I had a few tricks up my sleeve that I planned to use. *Thank you, Lupe brothers!* I mean, in theory, as long as I was able to wield them without impacting my own men. I had tested a bit of the cloudy film Sandro had told me about, sending out a fog of confusion, hoping that I was lowering the guard of...well...the guards, but based on the shitty instructions I'd gotten from Sandro, I had no idea if it was working or if I was simply pushing around nothing but false hope. Lore's shared gifts? That was a whole lot trickier to toss around. I wasn't even quite sure how to tap into them, which was a problem for another day.

I had the backing of a shit-ton of wolves in Italy now, so if things went sideways, I felt I'd have some fighting chance.

We'd arrived at dawn, just as the forest was waking up to the day creatures — the night beasts having skulked away already, probably because they sensed our approach and knew better than to stick around.

The compound itself jutted from the hills of Bellagio, as if it had grown out of the ground like the trees surrounding it. It was tiered, four stories, giving it an ancient building blocks kind of look, like a child had plopped huge slabs of rock zigzag into the hills. The stones had aged into a camouflage that matched the woods around it, moss edging the blocks and ivy growing up the centers.

If it wasn't for the pompous display of statues in the likeness of each of the scholars, I assumed, it could pass unnoticed. As it was, there appeared to be one way in, down a cobbled pathway, a gamut of guard wolves standing sentry all the way to the double stone doors.

I'd decided to bring an entourage, since I knew that the scholars were aware of my presence in Italy. Surely, they'd already heard rumors of my arrival in Bellagio. The rogue wolves that had been sniffing around the cathedral had likely been paid well for the information they'd brought here.

Hence the guard wolves. I doubted this was a normal display of power since, usually, the scholars had nothing to fear.

Until now.

Staying in my human form, I led a few choice members of my newly acquired pack toward the entrance. Levi and Johnny were at my sides, of course, Sandro and Lore near the back, as a show of possession, and the ones in between had been hand-picked by Robbie, who was now my right hand in Italy.

The guards all turned in unison the moment my foot stepped over the threshold marking the end of the forest trail and the beginning of the path to enlightenment—or so the sign said.

"You are not permitted to cross into this territory," the closest guard said, his voice deep and rumbly. He didn't make eye contact and stood three feet taller than me, so I could tell he thought intimidation would work. His arms were crossed, and he held no weapons, so I had to assume his posturing usually worked on most trespassers. I pushed what I thought was Sandro's powers out, hoping that I was at least somewhat projecting his persuasive fog to mingle with the rising mist.

"Is that because it's a weekend? Are the scholars off duty?" I popped up on my tiptoes, trying to catch his eyes, keeping my tone a little on the flirty side. "Or because I'm a woman? Because I heard a rumor that women weren't allowed inside the...well, you know"—I nodded toward the compound—"sacred space."

He averted his gaze but said nothing. Did he know about Lore's power? Did he sense it in me somehow?

"I don't think he knows who I am." I glanced over at Johnny, who was doing his damnedest to keep a smirk off his face...and failing completely. "Honey, didn't you let the scholars know I was coming?"

"You will leave the premises immediately." The guard ordered, taking a step so he was all up in my space. "You have no business here."

"Oh, you're wrong about that." I moved forward, too, changing my height by letting a little of my werebeast loose. Now we were chest to chest, and there was nowhere else he was looking but directly into my eyes. "I don't want to hurt you or your men, but if you don't get out of my way, I'm going to rip your throat out."

I let my fangs drop and shivered through a split-second shift that had me in full beast before he could blink.

His mouth opened, then closed, his eyes wide, pupils pinpricks. "Y-y-y-you're..."

His men broke rank behind him, moving farther rather than closer. He gave a shaky glance over his shoulder but didn't order them back into position.

I leaned in to press my fangy mouth to his ear. "Let's pretend you put up a fight." I wrapped my hand around his throat, my fur trailing in the sweat beading from his jaw. "I won't tell anyone." I leaned my body closer, pressing into him so he could feel the strength of my rippling muscles. "Do you really want to give up your life for them?"

"No, my queen." His eyes were steady, shining sincerity. He was totally not fucking with me.

What the actual...? Did every goddamn werewolf on this planet know who I was?

"Step away." He started to but I held his throat. "Better yet, go away. I don't want to see you again."

He pulled back enough to look me in the eye. "I would serve you."

I growled. "After you've served these spineless fools? I'd never taint my pack with the likes of you." I pushed him aside, making him stumble to get out of my way. "Scatter, all of you," I said with a wave of my furry arm. "If I see you again, I'll tear you apart."

Much to my disappointment, the guards gave no further protest. They disappeared into the forest like ghosts.

"That was—"

"Way too easy," I finished for Johnny. We made eye contact, then both turned to look at Levi.

"There's magic here. Nothing that smells like a problem, but there is something different. One beat that doesn't match the rest of the pulses." Levi nudged me. "See what you can feel, Charlie. Open your senses a little more than you are. I'll steady you."

Along with the weird witchy werewolf magic, Lore and Sandro had also gifted me with some truly enhanced magic detecting abilities. The only problem was that magic was all over the fucking place in Italy. The country was doused in the stuff. Interesting, yes, but not something I wanted to explore with new abilities. I had to figure out pretty quickly how to clamp that shit down before I got overwhelmed, which I had done, somehow, at the cathedral.

So, I wasn't keen on doing what Levi asked, but I could see his point. The better I understood what was going on here, the more information I had, the quicker this would go.

And I needed things to happen quickly because Kane was waiting for me. Not literally, of course... Right this moment he was in England on his way to the master's compound to get some answers for me, according to Levi. But figuratively, I needed this Italy trip to wrap up so I could be one step closer to being with Kane.

I let myself shift back to my human form. The last thing I needed was to open myself up to magic and lose control over my baser instincts...which I assumed might happen, since all the magic floating around was drenched in werewolf essence...something my beastly self really, really liked in a 'murdery' kind of way.

Levi put his hand on my shoulder, a comforting weight as I closed my eyes and willed my senses to open slowly, carefully. A trickle of power flowed along my nerve endings, sparking curiosity but still being cautious. The flow of magic was a torrent behind the wall of my control. I felt the pulsing of it push against my awareness, questing for my full attention. I eased back, closing myself up and blocking out what wanted in.

"It's a lot," I said, knowing that Levi would want me to try again.

He squeezed my shoulder. *"I'm right here. Standing with you. I won't let it take you down."*

His voice in my head soothed my nerves. The pulse of confidence he surged through our bond gave me strength and courage.

I readied myself, bracing for a flood, then I opened myself up completely and let the magic cascade over me.

Levi's hand on my shoulder kept me from stumbling back as the power from layers of spells soaked into my awareness. It was primal magic, the trees around us teeming with it. It was in the dirt and air. It coated every inanimate thing and danced along my skin. The leaves on the trees seemed to sing with it, rustling vibrantly because of the lupine magic running through their veins.

I let the magic roll over my new awareness, separating it from what I was coming to learn was more common types of spells, clumsy in the face of whatever this was. I tested its edges, feeling for a start, a stop, and finding that it just continued outward, bouncing off of me, off Levi and Johnny and the wolves who had my back, to radiate away once again.

It was emanating from the building in front of me. Within the walls of the scholar's compound there was an ancient magic that drew me forward — a halting step that made my whole body shiver.

"There is something distinctly female about what I'm feeling," Levi whispered, awe laced in his words. "You know what I mean?"

"Yes," I croaked, because the pieces were coming together — missing scrolls and untold stories, a longing so deep that my heart ached. I took another step closer, drawn in by the feeling of loneliness. It was female. Hard to say how, but there was a pulse of familiarity, a likeness to my own essence that made it distinctly not male.

Which made no sense since it was well known that the scholars were always men — the smartest, not necessarily the strongest, of our kind. The scholars protected our history, uncovered our legacy…or so I'd been taught all my life.

A female presence meant one thing to me, and it ignited my fury in an explosion. They had a captive.

I roared my displeasure at the realization that they had a prisoner inside, a strong female who had been somehow subdued. Her essence was everywhere, laced in the magic all around us. My beast instincts took over, and I bulked up in an instant, losing myself in the magic that was all around me. I charged to the stone doors that lay ahead.

The thud of paws behind me told me that I was supported. I wouldn't be entering the compound alone, not that I was worried. I'd rip into anyone who stood in my way. My pack aligned with me, bolstered me, pushed me through any fear I felt, tempered me against the wrath I wanted to lay down.

"Seek first to understand…" Levi's voice in my head echoed. *"Blood will come later."*

I ran full tilt, ready to slam the doors down to get inside…and had to skid to an abrupt stop, claws digging in, leaving long divots as I tried to dispel the momentum I'd accumulated so I didn't slam into the figure that emerged as the doors swung open.

I stopped inches from her, my chest heaving, breath whooshing out in hard pants, towering over an elderly female—a werewolf, a powerful one.

She tilted her face to meet my gaze and smiled. "Well now, you are impressive, aren't you?"

Chapter Eighteen

Johnny

"Ho-ly shit!" I couldn't help blurting the first thing that came to my head. This woman, hunched, frail, white hair cascading in angry knots down her back, who somehow looked more bohemian than feral, was an elder. A female alpha to be sure, wild in her expression, withered fangs poking past her dry lips, she'd seen centuries for sure. "I thought you were all dead," I said to no one, to everyone, my mouth gaping — shock like a fog making my brain stutter over what my eyes were seeing.

"He's not the bright one, is he?" The old woman gave me a once-over that was full of suggestion and just as shocking as her existence. She licked her lips like I was a piece of meat cooked to her liking then she winked. I couldn't help but grin. "No offense. Sometimes the looks are all that matter." Her eyes danced with mischief.

She's feisty. I liked her already.

"You're an ancient," Levi said, like this wasn't the shock of our lives to see a living, breathing female werewolf with faded black swirled marks etched over her throat and up her jaw. She'd been marked and had, presumably, given marks, just as Charlie had.

"Ancient…" She smirked. "That, I am." She lifted a hand to Charlie. "Not a direct ancestor to you, queen, but one with a story to tell. You come seeking answers. I have them."

Charlie, still in beast form, uncharacteristically, took the old woman's hand, not to shake but to stroke, like she was in awe, just as I was. Her touch was gentle, tentative, comical, considering she was all fur, claws and muscle while this ancient werewolf was anything but.

It was a display of affection from Charlie that I hadn't expected but that seemed appropriate. The old woman flipped Charlie's hand then ran her clawed finger along the pad of her beastly palm, following her lifeline reverently. She nodded like she was seeing something she expected to see.

"I came seeking retribution," Charlie admitted, her voice hoarse. "I wasn't expecting to find you."

"Of course, on both counts." Her laugh was gnarled like her throat was coated with rivets. "What I have to say might alter your plans." She flipped Charlie's hand over, holding it at eye level. "Depends how stubborn you are."

Very. Stubborn. Went without saying.

Charlie looked over her shoulder at Levi, not seeking permission but confused all the same. Did we want to hear what this ancient had to say? Did we want to alter our plans?

Charlie's beast eyes shimmered.

While her head was turned, the ancient dropped her hand, shrugged then turned.

"Come or don't. I'm not going to beg." Then she disappeared into the darkness beyond the entrance. "Close the door either way. The bugs are horrendous this time of year."

"This feels once in a lifetime." Charlie shook her head, obviously fighting herself with indecision. "But it could be a trap."

"I'm not detecting anything we can't handle." Levi looked at me. "Johnny?"

"I'm the stupid one, remember?" I grinned to let them know I hadn't taken the old woman's words seriously. "Let's see what she has to say."

"And the scholars?" Charlie frowned, her beastly muzzle contorting in a way that made me want to laugh and kiss her. I held back because I didn't want to lose my head. She was in no mood for fooling around.

"Would she be here, walking free, if there was a problem with the scholars?" Levi said.

"No, I guess not." Charlie sighed as she transformed to her human self. "Unless it *is* a trap," she mumbled.

She waved to the men behind us at the same time that she sent a jolt down our collective treads. We were all connected to Charlie in one way or another, so her reassurance followed by *stay cautious and alert*, was a ripple that shook each of us in turn. With a meaningful look at Levi and I, she ordered the rest of the pack to stay behind.

No one argued, of course, but Levi and I shared a look that could have been construed as oppositional by a more ego-sensitive alpha. We both knew that once those thick stone doors closed, it would be hard for our men to get inside—not impossible, but definitely difficult. Charlie knew it, too, and she was ordering us in anyway.

"Let's go." Charlie didn't wait for us, leaving our doubts behind as she headed into the maw of the compound with no hesitation.

I shrugged, Levi beelined right after her. The old alpha hadn't said we couldn't accompany our mate. She had to have known we'd go wherever Charlie went. I motioned to the rest of the men to keep their eyes on our surroundings, then followed Levi and Charlie into the darkness. I instantly detected the lingering scent of Kane, hours old but strong enough to tell me he'd been at least this far into the compound.

And he hadn't met the old werewolf queen. He would have told us if he had.

Interesting. She'd kept herself hidden while he'd been here. Why?

Because she wanted Charlie and only Charlie. Made me wonder how much of our experiences so far had been orchestrated to get Charlie here.

My eyes adjusted to the limited light, and I couldn't help but appraise the priceless antiques in the foyer. The floor was polished obsidian, bouncing the reflection of hundreds of flameless candles set in original iron candelabras. I chuckled at the modern upgrade. Vancouver humans would absolutely kill for stone like this, and the aged iron with centuries of patina would go for thousands at the artesian markets I loved so much. The walls were roughly carved stone, gray and brown that looked like someone had taken a pitchfork to tunnel into the mountain, which they probably had...werewolf style. There wasn't a type of rock that a strong pair of claws couldn't carve with enough dedication.

I guessed a lot of wolf hours had gone into creating this place, and because of that, I felt an instant calm roll over me. Not magic, like Lore and Sandro attempted to force on me, more like a homecoming that came with a certain level of innate comfort. I noticed that both Charlie and Levi seemed more relaxed, too. Their shoulders weren't riding as high to their ears as when they'd first entered the compound, and their vibrations, the virtual hackles I was attuned to, were down enough to put me at ease.

Charlie didn't seem to need a guide through the main foyer. She walked with confidence down the hall, bypassing tunnels that jutted in different directions to the east and west. My curiosity piqued with each dark pathway we passed, echoes of werewolf voices that felt more like imprints from centuries ago rather than current residents, tickled along my senses. This place was haunted, to be sure, and I hoped I'd be given the chance to explore later.

"You know what they say about curiosity." The old woman's raspy laugh came out of the dim light ahead. "But you're no cat, my queen."

"Charlie, if you don't mind," Charlie said as we entered the room the old woman was in—a sitting room slash library with bookshelves carved into the stone walls and bear-fur rugs, authentic by the smell of them, covering the floor.

"Oh, I know who you are, Charlotte Larsen," the old woman said. "You're the making of a legend."

"And you are?" Levi, ever the formal one, sounded like he was an ambassador for Charlie, stepped ahead of her to inspect the room. Also, knowing Levi, to sniff out if there was any magic at play he needed to protect us from.

The she-wolf cocked her head in his direction, watching him carefully as he scanned the room. "You should know who I am," she said as she turned her gaze back to Charlie, "if I know my great, great, great, so on and so forth." She waved her hand to denote more greats. "Nonetheless, grandsons, you'll have seen my likeness on a wall —"

"Wha?" Charlie gasped, then squinted, securitizing the woman's face. "How can that be?" She turned to me, her expression all disbelief. "She's centuries old...like more than normal..." Charlie looked back to the woman. "Vassa?"

"Seems impossible, doesn't it?" She waved a hand like it was no big deal for her to be here, alive, far longer than she should have been. "If you're picking up on any magic, sir, it's coming from me." She motioned the length of her body. "I believe you call it stasis? Magically induced."

She had Levi's full attention now.

"I have lived far longer than should be possible," Vassa said with a wry smirk. "Good genetics, although you can see that my body did take some aging hits." She flexed her fingers and the bones cracked and snapped. "I wasn't in my prime when we decided I needed to take some time out of the living world."

"Why, though?" Charlie blurted. "I mean, don't get me wrong. This is truly amazing. I'm so grateful to meet you, but why do this to yourself? It can't be...comfortable. You're, what, six hundred years old?"

"No, comfort wasn't the point, though, was it?" Vassa sighed like we were all beyond stupid. "The prophecy said you'd come."

"Did it say that you'd lose all your power? That the females would be hunted? That—"

"In a way, Charlie, yes, it did." Vassa cut her hand through the air like she was ending the discussion. "But that's not the point."

"Because it couldn't be stopped," Levi said. His expression was like a child with an unexpected present in front of him. He understood something that I didn't grasp, not at all. "You had to wait until the time was right. You agreed to stasis in order to reach this point of meeting Charlie."

Vassa nodded.

Charlie sucked in a breath, no doubt comprehending just how important she was.

"Why you?" Levi asked.

"Because I was the chosen one then, just as Charlie is the chosen one now." Vassa motioned to the chairs spattering the room. "Will you people sit down? You're making me agitated. We're not expecting a battle, are we? You men are amped to the tits." She chuffed a little, not impressed with us in the least. "Sit yourselves down or go outside and get your energy out."

I laughed, couldn't help it. It barked out of me like a strangled cough. I didn't make her demand it again. I swooped down into a chair, my back to the wall, just as Levi did the same thing, keeping the one and only visible door in our sightlines.

Vassa gave one of her sighs but didn't comment on our continued vigilance. She gave Charlie an expectant look, which got my mate moving double-quick. She seated herself next to Vassa in a large wingback that might have been big enough to support her in her beast form.

"I've heard a lot of words used to describe me since I met the Duke brothers but 'chosen one' hasn't been mentioned," Charlie said. "What does it mean?"

"It means that you come from a long line of warriors, child. And you're destined to turn the tide, just as I had been. Our world moves in cycles. This isn't the first time we've been hobbled, discounted, thrust aside. We are entering a time to hijack, a moment in the cycle when we can rise up and change the pattern — centuries ahead of when it would naturally occur."

"Sandro and Lore —"

"Are now your soldiers." She curled her lip, half smile, half sneer. "The fools couldn't control themselves."

"I'm sorry." But Charlie's tone didn't match her words.

"No, you're not. Don't degrade yourself by ever uttering those words to me again." Vassa cut through the air again with her hand. "You did what needed to be done, and now we're family of sorts...as foretold."

A swarm of cloaked werewolves entered carrying trays of glasses, a pitcher of water, wine, finger foods, pastries that made my mouth water. *Italian food... Give me all of it.*

Levi's mouth gaped as he watched the obvious servants deposit the trays then exit without a word. "These are the scholars?"

"My men." Vassa nodded. "Yes, they know their place."

"You've marked them?" Charlie sounded just as shocked.

Made sense to me. We hadn't seen them yet, so I'd assumed the scholars were either dead or bitten.

"Centuries ago. Part of the plan." She snatched a cannoli then shoved it into her mouth. "They kept me hidden. Kept the ruse going while I waited."

"They destroyed the scrolls," Charlie said, frowning. "Upholding the patriarchy. The old beliefs."

"You're not listening, Charlie." Vassa wiped her mouth with the back of her hand. Crumbs fell to her lap. "They were doing my bidding. Keep the ones in power believing in their power, unprepared for what was to come—your birth, my rising. The scrolls are meaningless."

"Meaningless?" Levi choked on air. "How can you say that?"

"Scrolls are merely interpretations of what could be," Vassa said. "What *may* unfold. But our lives are filled with choices. For a long time, our world has been governed by the males. But, as I've been trying to tell you, those times are changing."

"I don't understand." Charlie rubbed her forehead. "My father... The masters..."

"The masters are misguided. They thought they were doing right. Can't blame them, really. It was their time to rule in their way." Vassa put her hand on Charlie's knee. "Now it's *our* time."

Charlie looked at Vassa. Levi looked at me. I shrugged. The cannoli were delicious.

"You don't think you're the only one?" Vassa laughed.

"There are others? Like me?" Charlie snapped her eyes back to Levi.

He looked just as lost as she did.

I grabbed a lobster tail, powdered sugar getting on my pants.

"Hidden… Out there… Yes. You're the catalyst. You'll start the tsunami. The rest will follow." Vassa shifted the tray my way and motioned to a folded pastry at the far side. "The queen of queens."

It was filled with chocolate, the folded pastry melting on my tongue. *So much butter!*

"So, what you're saying"—Levi leaned forward, steepling his hands under his chin—"is that this is the dawn of a new world order."

"Yes." She nodded. "I like that. New world order." She took one of the chocolate delights then popped it into her mouth. With closed eyes, clearly relishing the delicacy, she continued, "But first, you have to understand the powers you possess—and how you'll harness them against your stepbrother."

"Sandro and Lore felt he was just a nuisance." Charlie didn't sound certain of that.

Vassa rolled her eyes. "They underestimate his hunger for power. He can still determine your destiny if you allow it. It's possible to lose to him, but you must not. The stakes are higher than you know. The others, they need you to rise, to beat down this prolific hunter who has ended ancestry lines of female werewolves who had been destined usurpers. He knows what he's doing. He knows your worth."

"And if I fail?"

"There will be no second coming, no chance to change the pattern. We'll have shown our hand. He'll come for me once he's taken everything he needs from you—your power, your knowledge, your connections and threads and bonds. If he gets those from you, he'll take from me and find the others." She tapped her head. "I'm the only one who knows everything, and once he finds out I exist, our world ends with me. He'll complete the genocide that was started in my day."

"He'll play dirty." Charlie sat up straight, harnessing her badass conviction, letting Vassa know that she was up for the challenge.

"Yes. We have to prepare you." Vassa plucked another pastry. "And it's not going to be fun."

Chapter Nineteen

Charlie

I was ready for sweat, blood, maybe, if something got severely broken, a few tears shed. I wasn't ready for the mind fuck that Vassa had planned when she said she had to prepare me for Sal.

Sure, my stepbrother was one nasty motherfucker, but what Vassa was putting me through wasn't training for my encounter with Sal, not the physical confrontation I knew was coming. She wasn't taking me through drills or strategizing a plan. She wasn't testing my reflexes or harnessing the power of my beast.

That, she said, was on me.

"You're not concentrating," she barked from her perch above me, her voice like a whip.

Like fuck I'm not!

"My head feels like it's going to explode," I mumbled, even as I bore down on my new powers.

"Your range is for shit, queen." Vassa waved her arms like I couldn't see her on top of the spiral staircase that led to the second floor of the library. "I'm hardly feeling a blip."

After taking me through a few poorly explained warm-up exercises, she'd climbed the staircase without the help of a couple of scholars who'd been fretfully hovering, then had cheerfully ordered me to hit her with everything I had.

I didn't know at the time just how badly I wished I could. The woman was relentless in her insults and had recently decided that words weren't enough of a motivator. She'd taken to throwing whatever was handy for me to dodge.

This time, a sculpture that, by the sound of it hitting the desk to my left, was made of some kind of heavy metal. Considering my eyes had been closed at the time that she threw it, I was not feeling very willing to participate in her way of doing things anymore.

I snarled at her, ready to bite her head off, literally, if she pushed me to.

"You're never going to beat Sal if you can't play dirty like he will." Vassa's voice was a steel grate against my ears. "You need to set him up for failure. Create a space that will trap him."

So far the amount of space I'd be able to trap him in would be the equivalent to a small washroom...maybe a pantry.

I doubted I could lure him into the Duke mansion with the scent of Levi's cooking...no matter how delicious it always was.

A book went flying past my head, wisping against my cheek before hitting the wall behind me. "See?

You're not even paying attention! Get your mind in the game, queen! Stop daydreaming!"

"I'm fucking trying!" I roared as I clenched my fists, my jaw, my teeth then forced what little control I had over my new power, what little understanding I had of its parameters, out like a balloon, just as she'd told me at the start of this shitshow. The magic was sticky, unwieldy, like bubble gum and glue mixed together. It didn't want to spread, and it latched on to everything between me and where I wanted it to go. I shoved at it, using invisible hands to coax it farther outward, filling it with the suggestion of air to spread into the space, which was hard to do when you didn't really understand how something worked. Vassa had assured me that this was the way. This was how she'd been taught, although she was probably conveniently forgetting the fact that she'd been born with it and therefore had a natural affinity built in.

I pushed harder, and when it popped, which it had done each and every time, it knocked me back fast enough to send me sprawling, so I crashed into a wooden chair that had no business being so flimsy. It splintered into a dozen pieces, and I felt like I was coated in goop.

I lay among the wreckage, cursing myself, my stupid new powers, my overall ineptitude.

"You're not even coming close to trying." Vassa grunted as she moved down the stairs, something I was sure her scholars would be upset she was attempting alone. With all her insults hurled at me over the last few hours, I didn't feel like peeling myself off the floor then rushing to help her.

She seemed fine and, I knew by now, stubborn enough to take insult if I even tried to help.

"You're a mess," she said after she'd shuffled over to peer down at me. "And you're blocked up."

"Blocked up?" I pushed onto my elbows and squinted at her. I hadn't done a full, Kane-style workout with this woman, but I felt exhausted all the same.

"There's something stopping you from letting go with this magic." She tapped her finger to her chin as if she hadn't already planned what she wanted to say next. "You don't trust it. You don't trust yourself."

Before I could argue, she held out her hand. "Come on. Let's break for tea. I need to hydrate. These old bones get dusty fast."

I was too tired to fight. I took her hand and let her think she was heaving me up, then was surprised by the reality that she did, in fact, heave me up, so fast actually that I bounced onto my tiptoes.

She gave me a look that said, *don't test me, girl*, then walked off to the other side of the room, a swish in her step like she wasn't hundreds of years past her prime. Her scholars were already entering—summoned by their bond to her, no doubt—with trays of teacups, a carafe, finger foods, more pastries. I silently hoped that Johnny was getting his fill of all the Italian delicacies he desired while I worked my ass off.

"You're burdened by something," Vassa started after we'd poured our tea and taken seats across from one another, a small oval table between us. It felt quaint and totally didn't vibe with my exhaustion. "Give it to me. What's on your mind?"

My mouth dropped open. Was this woman for real? *What's on my mind?* A shitload of things. "Is this a therapy session?"

"Call it whatever you'd like. You're stuck. I'm going to get you unstuck." She leaned forward, eyes full of don't-fuck-with-me. "Quit being so damn stubborn. I stayed alive for you, queen. I let myself get like this." She motioned up and down her body. "Show some damn respect and tell me what the hell is going on."

It was a slap in the face that had me sitting straight, my spine ramrod stiff, and suddenly infused with energy.

A therapy session it would be, then.

"Don't make me wait," she grumbled.

"What's on my mind?" I ran my hand down my face, trying to scrub the emotion away. No luck, I welled with frustration, a burst of it that made me blurt out my next words. "How about I came to Italy to get my third and ended up inheriting a load of werewolves, some powerful and foreign magic—which I can't even wield—and a whole lot of sexual frustration."

"I don't appreciate the sass, queen." There was no heat in her voice as she sipped her tea. "You've got other mates who can take care of your needs." She glanced at the door to indicate my men then swung her narrowed gaze back to me. "You're heartsick?"

Heartsick. I wanted Kane with me. I hated that he left, even if I understood why he had.

"I feel deprived." It was hard to admit my deepest feelings to a practical stranger. "Like a part of my heart is incomplete." I wouldn't give her tears, but I couldn't help the croak in my voice. "Kane left."

"He did what he needed to do." She refilled her teacup then picked it up, her pinky poised like a proper lady. "That's not it, though. That's not what's blocking you." She motioned with her other hand. "Go on. It isn't the magic or the werewolves you've adopted, either. You revel in that kind of power, even if you don't fully understand it all yet."

She wasn't wrong. It was a lot of responsibility to have taken on all the wolves I had, but it felt right…doable. The magic, while frustratingly hard to click with, didn't set me on edge as much as it felt like a challenge to conquer.

I knew what was really bothering me, and I didn't want to say it out loud. It was weak, pathetic—by werewolf standards, anyway.

"I know you're chewing on something. Just spit it out," Vassa said.

Ruby. She was my hang-up. "I ruined my best friend's life."

"A female?" Vassa's frown told me everything I already knew. Werewolves had no friends. They had family. They had packmates.

"Like a sister," I added.

"A human female?" She practically spat those words.

"She was bitten." I hated the gut turning mess in my stomach. I hated the look on Vassa's face, one of pure disgust. "She was going to die." I hated that I felt like I was making excuses. "You don't understand. You're—"

"Enough, girl," Vassa snapped. "I understand loyalty. That's what I hear in your voice." She sighed. "You bit her, saved her life. You're loyal. Your guilt is unfounded. Weak, dis—"

"She's barren now." I snapped, more venom in my tone than I meant. "She hates me."

"And you, queen, are worried about *that*? Losing a *friend*?" She scoffed in a not very therapist kind of way. "You have to be tougher than that if you're going to be the queen of queens."

"The guilt—"

"A human problem, not a werewolf one." She shook her head, showing me the disappointment she so clearly felt. "Your insecurity could cost all of us a future. Does that not have impact?"

"I didn't know about that until I came here." It was a poor excuse but one I felt needed to be said. "I've known Ruby for years. She was there for me when I was alone, ousted from my own clan." And that was it right there. I'd been abandoned. Had lost everything that had mattered to me. My father had died. The grief had overwhelmed me. Then my family had let me walk away.

The sorrow I had been pushing deep down came bubbling up, flooding my body so I slumped against the weight of it all. I stared at the floor, fighting the tears that burned the backs of my eyes.

"Being a lone wolf, even temporarily, is the worst kind of punishment." Vassa's tone had changed. She was suddenly softer...quieter.

Which was worse than her sharp voice. It made the tears roll down my cheeks in an embarrassing way. I scrubbed my sleeve across my face, sucked the emotion back into the hole I'd created for it.

"You were that desperate for female friendship that you latched onto a human and got attached." She *tsked*, but not in a scolding way. "It would have been different had you been surrounded by budding queens like yourself."

"As if that were an option," I snorted, covering my discomfort with sass once again. I wanted to get us back on safe footing. The therapy session was over, as far as I was concerned.

"It could be...if you succeed." Vassa took the hint and adjusted her voice back to business. "You won't succeed if you let this human burden you so much that you doubt yourself. That's what we'll need to break out of you."

I didn't disagree. I also didn't know how to stop feeling guilty for ruining Ruby's life. Because I had... I'd destroyed her world, her dreams, her future.

"When I bit her, I was going on my beastly instinct." If we were going to get to the bottom of things, I needed to be honest—and I honestly didn't feel like I'd made a mistake in saving Ruby's life. I might wish it didn't have consequences of making her barren, but I definitely couldn't stand to watch her die. I met Vassa's eyes, giving her the same bold look she was giving me. "The masters taught me how to cage my beast, and when I finally let her out, let her have control, she guided me to action."

"And what's your instinct telling you to do now?" She put her teacup down then leaned closer. "Have you even bothered to listen?"

I'd been too busy trying to harness power I didn't understand to turn inward—which, I realized, was exactly Vassa's point.

When I didn't answer, she cocked an eyebrow. "I bet it's telling you that I'm right. I bet your gut is urging you to let it go, to unleash your beast and give in to your new power."

My stomach fluttered like a horde of bees had taken flight. The beast parts of me perked up, came online, started paying attention. Where had she been this whole time? Back in her cage? Had I compartmentalized again?

"I bet it's telling you to step up, embrace the magic, trust it, let it do its thing," she continued.

She wasn't wrong. I did feel those things. I let that awareness build. I embraced those parts of me that wanted the most basic of things, those instincts beyond my werewolf self, the beastly drive, primordial understanding, infusing my heart with desire for power while balancing against my other needs — loyalty, love, family.

"You know how I know?" She tapped her head. "I have it, too." She laughed. "Not as powerful as you do. I didn't suck down the life force of two magically gifted, foolish males by biting them." She laughed harder, nearly doubled over in her seat.

Somewhat surprising, considering she was talking about her descendants.

Her laughing tapered off into coughing. She drank down the rest of her tea before continuing. "I knew fear once…so much fear that it stopped me in my tracks." She was all business once again. "Because of that, I never reached my full potential."

It was hard to imagine this woman in front of me being caught up in fear. Even in her frail-looking condition now, centuries old, I would trust her to stand with me if battle broke. I knew she'd fight to her death with everything she had.

"Your friendship is a liability." She raised her hand for me to shut up before I'd even opened my mouth to argue. "She's your responsibility now, and she, like all females, need you to rise up and take your destined place. Do you think Sal will stop at you? Do you think he won't kill your friend, too?"

If I was being honest, I hadn't considered anything beyond my own burdens for a long time.

Shame took over where guilt had dominated. I was alpha to hundreds. I was destined to be a queen. "How do I let go of the guilt? She didn't ask to be made one of us. I didn't ask for her consent. I didn't give her a choice." And that, too, was a human sentimentality.

For werewolves it came down to life or death.

Vassa's expression said it all. Life was always the choice. A queen would embrace that.

Thankfully, Vassa didn't bother to rip another strip off me. "She's mad at you? She hates you? Those are luxuries she doesn't get to have anymore. She's in a pack. Her human sensibilities need to go. You know this. If they don't, she'll die. You bit her, you own her, she answers to you." Her words were harsh, but also true. "You give your underling a purpose and put her to work. She's a wolf now, and she needs direction."

A knock at the door startled me out of our conversation. I cursed myself for being so caught up in Vassa that I hadn't even scented my mate approaching.

Levi poked his head in and flashed his phone. "Kane called."

My heart leapt. That was my other torment. I wanted to end this separation. I hated it, no matter how necessary it was.

"He's in England." Levi cleared his throat as he moved into the room. "Master's training center."

I frowned. There was something wrong. Levi's expression was roiling with barely tempered rage.

"They've scattered." Levi shook his head. "The cowards."

Of course they had. I'd have to hunt them down one by one later. Frustration rattled through me. There'd be no quick reckoning.

"What did they leave behind, son?" Vassa asked.

I narrowed my eyes. Levi's eyebrows jolted into his hairline.

"Spit it out. We don't have all day," Vassa barked.

"They had pups," Levi said, his eyes on me, his voice growly. "Females. All ages, but none over thirteen."

I gasped, snapped my gaze to Vassa. "How did you—?"

"Give your friend a purpose," she said, a nudge to a desperately needed solution.

"What do we do?" Levi asked. "I don't think we can delay heading home. Sal's making moves—"

"Make arrangements for us to fly home." I nodded at Vassa. I understood what needed to happen, what I had to do. I turned to Levi, putting my forgotten teacup down. "Tell Kane to meet us at home once backup gets to him in England." I stood, ready to finally accept my role. "Send Ruby and the boys to the master's compound. Tell her that she's a den mother now by order of her alpha."

Chapter Twenty

Charlie

"Vince is dead." I felt our accountant turned co-conspirator's murder on the flight back to Vancouver. Chest-ripping pain told me that my stepbrother had found out I'd turned one of his go-to guys into a double agent. As much as I didn't want to feel the agony of one of my own being killed — especially one who I loathed as much as I loathed my stepbrother — I refused to turn down the pain. I'd bitten Vince. He was mine. I owed him, at least, the dignity of dying knowing I was with him through our bond.

There was no question that Sal had tortured Vince, but the death had been quick — not painless but not prolonged. It was enough to tell me that Vince had broken faster than a werewolf hunting prey. I had no doubt that Sal knew what I'd been up to.

Not that it mattered.

Vince had been a pawn. Anything he'd known, I'd wanted Sal to know, too. Vince's job had been to arouse Sal's suspicions, which I'd known he'd do in his fumbling way at some point, and to feed him information about a rift between Kane and his brothers. We wanted Sal to think we were scattered, disorganized and divided.

Now he did.

"We'll hold a vigil for all the fallen once this is over." Levi, as usual, was thinking logically. "No sense in pomp and circumstance right now."

Johnny gave me a side hug that I'd never admit I needed. I leaned into him when he started to pull away, and he curled his arm around my waist, holding me close.

We were seated on a cramped couch, flying home, Levi across a small table from us. We were all feeling the weight of our next actions, the deaths it would likely bring, casualties on both sides.

We had a plan that was filled with holes.

"Tell me again how you think Sal's spell will work?" I wanted to forget all this and nuzzle into Johnny's skin, inhale his scent, let him soothe me away from all of the strategy and diabolical plans.

"Well, we don't know exactly what he has planned after the spell takes hold," Levi said, his voice distracted as he sent orders to the many sets of wolves we'd need to pull our plans off. "But, in theory, Sal's spell will hold you in place."

"Like how Lore's spell worked on you guys?"

Levi had already gone through this with us, but there was a lot bugging me about the unknowns.

I hadn't asked that question the last time, so Levi glanced up from his computer, one eyebrow cocked.

"Um…kind of. It's a layered spell that the witches use a lot—one that ignites the other, like a chain reaction. In this case, if the legacy holds true, it will be Kane's bite, your third, that will be the catalyst."

We'd sent Vince to renegotiate the contract Kane had signed that he hadn't realized contained hidden witch text. Fine print that would put me in danger, a literal sitting duck, for my stepbrother to fulfill his darkest desires. He wanted to hunt the most powerful female werewolf in existence…which, apparently, would be me once Kane and I completed the triad.

"And me biting Kane." I felt compelled to say it, even though everyone knew the score.

All the same, everyone paused at the implication. Johnny's arm loosened around my waist. Levi's typing stopped.

Kane would be on his way to me as soon as Ruby took over at the master's abandoned compound. He'd be flying from England to Vancouver. My body registered his proximity, despite him being thousands of miles away. Whatever was pulsing through me to complete the triad would amplify the closer we got to one another. Part of me wanted to sit right on the runway and wait for Kane's flight to land, but that would mess up our plans.

"Right." Levi cleared his throat, pulling me from my thoughts. "Once you achieve that, with Kane, Sal's spell, in theory, will ignite."

There was something so unnerving about that. My stepbrother was waiting for me to unite with the third and final Duke brother so that he could hunt me down and murder me.

"But we don't know how strong of a spell it is," I confirmed, tearing my thoughts away from the brutality of my stepbrother's desires.

Levi nodded.

"So we don't know if it's a literal frozen in place kind of thing or a confined to a space kind of thing," Johnny said, his voice thick.

"No, but I think we can make some educated guesses based on what we know about Sal." Levi resumed his typing.

"That's he's a sadistic bastard," Johnny said. "And he loves to hunt."

Everyone knew the consequences of Sal succeeding in any part of his plans.

"Right." My gut was saying he'd want to confine me to a large enough space to give him sport. "The Duke compound is legendary for its expansive property lines." My father had always admired Kane's land acquisition. He'd seen so much forethought in Kane's planning, even when the other alphas mocked him for buying nothing but trees. They'd all been fighting one another for the limited space in the cities. The property the Duke mansion was situated on, while out of the way, was a hundred acres of mostly untouched forest and the perfect site for a large pack of werewolves to train and play—which they had…in preparation for my eventual arrival.

"Sal will consider it a double triumph if he defeats me on my own turf." *My own turf.* It was a reality that was still new enough to make me stutter on the thought of it. It had been a long time since I'd had a home among wolves, and the Duke mansion, with all its plentiful forest, was now mine.

"It would be a trophy for sure," Levi nodded, not even blinking at what I'd said—that I'd claimed the land along with their mating bond.

My heart doubled in size, filling with love and gratitude that I didn't know how to express without coming off as a lunatic.

These Duke men, they'd sought me out. They'd held on tight, even when I'd done whatever I could to push them away. They'd give up everything for me, even their lives.

I swallowed the boulder in my throat.

"So, Kane and I need to keep our shit together." Meaning no getting caught up in our passion or losing ourselves in each other. No matter how much we craved taking things all the way, it wasn't going to be easy to control our urges, especially when fangs were involved. "We need to be prepared for an attack as soon as the bite ignites the spell."

"No, I've bought you some time." Levi turned his computer to show me the screen. "I've got some guys working on creating delays, so Sal gets caught up in putting out other fires. It'll take him a while to realize you and Kane are back in Canada."

Kane's flight would be taking off within the hour, but there was a chunk of time—four hours to be exact—that I'd need to kill before I could get to him. Hard, but not impossible. I remembered what it had been like as a young pup waiting for gifts from my father. Patience was always rewarded.

If Levi had a way to keep Sal busy so Kane and I would have the luxury of a few extra moments together, I considered it a blessing.

Suddenly the black cloud that had been circling my mood for the last few hours broke and floated away.

I would have time with Kane. I'd be able to make our union as significant as it was. Kane had been evasive. He'd had his reasons to push me away. He'd wanted a traditional bonding, male to bite female. I'd thrown a major wrench in that plan, and he'd needed time to adjust to it. We would have our time together, and we'd make it special.

"Thank you," I whispered. I knew what it cost Levi to make accommodations so I could be with his brother.

"I haven't told Kane," Levi said, once again focused on his screen. "You'll connect with him, right?"

While there'd never been angry jealousy between the brothers, I had, on occasion, felt the sharp edge of playful competition going a bit too far. I knew they all vied for my attention. I knew any virile male would feel a possessive need to have their mate with him and not with anyone else. So, this was an act of generosity that reaffirmed our bonds. I knew it took a lot for Levi to set it up.

It felt like sunshine radiating to my heart. No permission sought but a quiet understanding that the next part of our journey would be devoted to Kane.

I nodded, unable to keep the smile from cracking my face wide open.

"I will." *Right now* went without saying.

Johnny tugged me closer, and I tilted my face up, taking in his steel eyes and the glint of aggressive need there. He wouldn't cover up his desires. Johnny was too pure for that. But when he ran his thumb along my jaw then kissed my forehead, I knew it was a blessing to do what I had to do.

I extracted myself from him—reluctant, while at the same time eager to connect with Kane. Even if we couldn't yet, physically, be together, I had other ways to get to him.

I put my hand on Levi's shoulder as I walked past him, and he clasped his over mine for the briefest of moments. It was enough of a connection to fill me with warmth all over again.

I left them in the lounge, knowing they'd be okay and made my way to the bedroom so I could have privacy. On the way, I slipped Kane's name into my thoughts, balling it up and tossing it into the ether, prodding him to pay attention...to get comfortable.

I was coming for him.

Chapter Twenty-One

You waited in the shadows, having heard my summons, stalking me from the darkness as I stepped into the muted light.

I wouldn't bother being coy. I'd willed myself naked, standing before you bare and vulnerable. Electricity tingled all over my body, my skin humming for contact.

You were on me in a heartbeat. You swept me up into your arms, your barrel chest crushing against my tits, radiating heat and power, your muscles rippling as you wrapped me up. You moved your hands along my spine, my waist, my hips, until you lifted me, coaxing my legs to grip your waist. My pussy pressed to your stomach, melting against your muscles.

I was frenzied, kissing your face, your jaw. The stubble that abraded my lips was welcome. The heat in my body flamed higher the more I rubbed along your stomach, the ridges of your abs a blessed friction.

You claimed my mouth roughly, nothing teasing about your kiss. You were taking, finally, no games, all want, giving in to the urges that had kept us apart, no words necessary. Your tongue was a dagger, jolting my mouth as you thrust, a welcome warning for what I wanted to come next.

You moved your hand between my legs, stroking along my slit, making me moan into your mouth, lips quivering, desperate for more.

I ran my fingers through your hair, gripping tightly as I hoisted myself up higher, your one hand on my ass holding me easily as you circled my clit with the tips of your fingers of your other hand.

I willed us onto a soft mattress of ether, calling more to surround us, giving you freedom to explore my body without having to keep us on our feet.

You didn't argue my choice and instead moved along my body, trailing fire over my jaw, down my throat. You nipped with fangs I so badly want to pierce me, scraping the tender skin without breaking through. I arched into you, pushing my flesh against your teeth, wishing we were together in real life instead of floating in my mind-created world. You grunted, a kind of purr as you sucked on my earlobe, then moved lower, over my collarbone, across my chest.

I slid my hands down your torso, tracing the valleys of your muscles, along the hard ridges of your stomach until you moved out of reach, your head dipping lower, igniting desire as you latched onto my nipple with your lips, your fingers still teasing my clit.

I bucked into you, begging for more. Don't make me wait this time.

Normally, that was exactly the game you'd play, torturing me for hours with your skillful fingers and roving lips. This time you're right there with me, as desperate for me as I was for you. You slipped down my body, not stopping until you were nestled between my legs, your molten eyes blazing as I looked down the hills of my body to see you working hard to devour my pussy.

You played with my nipples, fingers of both hands flicking and pinching so hard that I cried out.

I wanted you to stop. I wanted you to keep going.

You knew my body in this world. You knew what I needed, what I wanted.

My climax was a bullet train, speeding through my body, and you were relentless, invoking a beastly roar that slipped past my lips when I orgasmed hot and hard, a relentless pulse that shook my legs and made me press my body feverishly against your lips.

I quivered, goosebumps rising and my head in the fog surrounding us, lost to the pleasure.

You kissed up my sensitive skin, making me jolt. I squirmed, determined to endure the torture as you made your lazy way over each erogenous zone, teasing me with your lips until I was panting all over again.

When you finally reached my mouth and kissed me, I could taste my orgasm on your lips – a salty tang that made me hungry for your cock. I ran hands over your body as low as I could go until I latched onto your dick, taking your shaft into my palm – holding the weight, aching for you to slide into me.

Your guttural moan zinged through me, and an uncontainable smile slipped over my lips.

I love that sound.

When I started to move, following the same path over your jaw that you had with mine, you stopped me with a hand on my throat. I fought enough for you to squeeze, fingers wrapped tightly so I had to stop or risk choking myself. Locking eyes, yours calm and serious, you shook your head.

"Not yet," you growled.

"Why not?" Frustration welled, but you kissed it away with a laugh that turned into a moan. Your kiss was fire. I melted into your wishes.

"We're so close," you said, your voice a hoarse whisper as you pulled back to press your forehead against mine. "I want to wait."

"Kane," I whined, but your grip on my throat tightened again, enough to tell me you were back in Dom mode.

"We'll wait," you commanded. "No more release until we're together."

And because we were hours away from finally being together in real life, I sealed my lips. A silent agreement. I wouldn't indulge in any pleasure until it was with Kane.

You slipped fingers into my hair and brushed it away from my face, your expression patient, your eyes shining both want and something else, softness under your lava.

Your tenderness hit me in the heart, undoing me completely. You were right, though. We needed to wait. Our coming together would be in the real world, no more fantasy connections.

"We have a plan," I croaked, attempting to switch back to business mode...and failing. I was still naked, still pressed against your body, still aching for you to kiss me again.

You closed your eyes for a brief moment, and when you opened them again, the fire was gone. You pulled back, unlatching me from your body. "Tell me."

Chapter Twenty-Two

Kane

The impatience of having to wait through traffic to get to Charlie had me practically clawing my way through the door of the limo. "Can't we go any faster?"

The answer was no. The driver, Tom, was a werewolf I'd turned over a decade ago. He knew my moods like his own. He didn't bother to respond. I could see the bumper-to-bumper traffic just as well as he could.

"This is taking too long." I gripped the edge of the seat, my fingernails digging into the upholstery. "Get us off this highway."

With a quick glance at the GPS, Tom turned the wheel. "Hang on, boss," he bullied his way through the lanes of vehicles, earning us a lot of pissed off honks and angry gestures from other drivers until we finally reached the off ramp.

It would take us into the city where traffic would be marginally better, but I was counting on Tom to have a plan to get us through the worst of it quickly.

We hit another jam almost immediately, but Tom took us down a side street, then another, until we came out to another backed-up road.

"Fuck!" I slammed my fist into the ceiling and rattled the interior of the car. "I could run there faster."

Charlie's flight had landed two hours ago. She was waiting for me at the house, just as anxious to finish what we'd started in her dream world. I didn't need to see her face or feel her anxiety to know it matched mine.

My fangs ached in a way I'd never known before, not just a pulse to the beat of my rapid heart but a need to bite deep and fast, the flesh of my future mate calling to me.

We'd waited too long. For good reasons, yes, but I wouldn't be lying if I said, I was dying to sink into her. I knew she'd been preoccupying herself with setting up the trap for Sal, using her new powers to build a net so she could hold Sal on our property—a kind of poetic justice since that was what his spell was about to do to us. He thought he'd have us in his sights when really, Charlie would be the one turning the tide on his plans. At least, that's what I hoped would happen. Charlie hadn't been too confident in her ability to wield her power, and we were still iffy on whether or not Sal would fall into our trap.

Things to worry about later. Right now, I needed to be with Charlie…immediately.

"Go. Faster," I demanded, knowing I was being unreasonable. "Drive down an alley if you have to. Just get us there!"

Tom turned his attention away from the road, his eyebrows almost touching his hairline as he started to say something to me over his shoulder.

Out of the corner of my eye, I had a moment of warning, a dark shape barely registered, then the limo jolted, time slowed, sound stopped, my body was suspended for a split second and I could see the scene clearly like I was out of my body and looking down.

We'd been T-boned.

Time sped up, and sound tore through my ears. Screeching, twisting metal, grating against itself, as it crumpled in on us, sending us spinning sideways, only to be hit again, then spun around in the other direction.

My world exploded in pain, the smell of blood in my nose, coating my mouth, muscles tearing, bones crunching.

We kept moving, glass shattered all over, sliding along my skin while the car spun. No seatbelt would have held me, my bulk too much for the standards. I was flung to the side then slid along the roof, my neck bent, bones popping…exponential agony.

When the sound of chaos ended and the car stopped, all that was left was ringing in my ears and the inability to control my limbs.

Disoriented, I couldn't make sense of where I was. Somewhere on the floor, crumpled in a heap, my arms trapped in front of me, pinned by two seats. Tom's body lay like a broken puppet, the strings snapped, eyes open, unblinking. He wasn't dead. A car accident wouldn't kill a werewolf that easily, but he was defenseless until his body fused itself back together, just like I was. No matter how much I willed myself to extract my limbs from where I was, I couldn't command the healing to go faster.

The back door I was wedged against cracked open, wrenched by powerful hands that made the metal scream. My head flopped back, bones definitely broken, so I was looking at the sun, blinded by its intensity.

"There's the big man." Sal's voice was distant, a wave of sound. My eyes rolled farther back, but I couldn't see him.

Instinct kicked in, overriding the damage to my body. A shudder went through me as I tried to shift.

"Collar him," Sal ordered.

The cold metal was welcome support over my neck for a split second, offering strength to the bones that were shattered. The pure silver that it was made out of seeped into my flesh like it was shedding its metallic poison. Agony was too mild a word for the flames that scorched my throat. It stopped my breath and froze my heart, my roar cut short as the metal halted my shift. Through the torture came the hum of magic. It spiked into my spine like a hot poker, slim, sharp and debilitating to my werewolf. I was trapped — broken, bloodied, unable to heal.

Sal's face came into my line of sight, warped by the wafting power from the collar and the pain that clouded my sight. "I've waited for this day a long time, Kane." Sal laughed. "Get him out of here."

* * * *

"Kane." Charlie's voice sounded like it was underwater, echoing in my mind. For a few moments, I thought I was in her dream world somehow, not understanding why she'd make me feel so much pain.

"Kane! Wake up!"

Soft fingers, tender touches, lifted my face as I fought to crack my eyes open. It was like prying open a vault.

"He's waking up." Charlie's tone was urgent. "I have to bite him."

No…no, Charlie. Get away. Run.

"You'll have to get that collar off him first," Levi said.

"No," I croaked. "Don't."

"He's delirious," Charlie said. "Help me move him."

Hands tugged under my arms, an attempt to lift me. "No!" I roared, hoping it sounded better than it did in my head. "It's a trap!"

"No shit, bro," Johnny laughed. "Quit fighting us."

"Stupid. Leave. Me." Each word stuck to my tongue, my throat on fire with the collar's vibration.

"Who are you calling stupid?" Charlie huffed in my ear before kissing me there. "Shut up, macho man."

She ran her hands along my jaw, then, before I could fight or argue, slipped her fingers under the collar, wedging her flesh between the poison and my skin.

She hissed, sucking in a deep breath, still close to my ear so I knew she was taking on the agony that I'd been enduring. The magic receded, pulling back with each huff of air she let loose from her lips. My body began to relax, falling into arms that were ready for me, helping me to the ground as Charlie moved with me. I knew, on some level, that she was using new powers to help me—powers I didn't understand.

Despite how torn up my skin was, I felt her shift her hands to beastly ones, the fur tickling me in a strangely comforting way. She grunted as she used her partial shift to rip the metal in two, yanking the pieces of the collar apart then throwing them to land with a clang somewhere in the room.

She moved my head to her lap as she settled on the ground with me. She stroked my hair and nuzzled the side of my face. Firm hands roved over my body, prodding and poking, hitting sore spots that made me grit my teeth.

"You're going to be okay," Charlie said, her hair dangling over my face as she stared down at me.

My sight was hazy still, but her eyes shone like emeralds, and I believed whatever she was saying.

"His spine is broken," Levi said. "Damn, all his ribs are fractured. Punctured something that's bleeding still. He's in bad shape."

"Not for long." Charlie brushed her hand down my chest. "Leave us, please."

There was no argument when there should have been. We had no time for this. She needed to get the hell out of here.

I heard the chuff of shoes walking away and cursed under my breath.

"Charlie," Levi said from farther away, "we're on borrowed time."

"Leave. Us." Charlie growled.

She waited until she heard the door click before moving—lifting my head from her lap and lowering me to her arm so I was cradled still, my neck supported. She moved alongside me, nestling her body close to mine, her breath just under my jaw.

"Sal—"

"Don't say his name right now." Charlie ran gentle fingers along my jaw then down my throat. "I'm going to torture him just for this alone."

I winced as she hit the raw wound left from the collar.

"How did you find—?" I coughed, words clogging my voice.

"A message was sent." She kissed where my wounds still burned. "A location where to find you."

"Trap?" I was lost to her touch, her fingers roving over my chest as she pressed her lips more urgently to my skin.

"Yes." She opened my shirt then slipped her hand along my pecs.

"We should—"

"Shhhhh," she cooed, moving her tongue over my skin.

"Charlie—" I moaned when her fangs scraped along my collarbone, her kisses becoming fiercer as she traveled as far as her pinned arm would allow.

"It's time, Kane." She opened her mouth on my chest, letting me feel the sharpness of her teeth. She'd take her bite over my heart, a fitting place to mark me. "Is this what you want?"

I swallowed, unable to move my head to nod, words all tangled up in my throat. When she looked up to meet my eyes, she got her answer.

With a deeply wicked grin that made my dick ache, she lowered her head and pierced me with her fangs.

The connection was instantaneous, and her power flowed into me like a torrent. Muscles healed, bones fused together, pain disappeared, vison cleared, and I could move my body again. She was even more powerful than I'd ever thought.

I gripped her head, pulled a startled yelp from her as I yanked her up my body, bringing her face to face with me.

"Take it easy. You're still healing," she laughed.

I kissed her concern away, roving her mouth with my tongue, my fangs already getting in the way.

She rolled her body over mine and rubbed herself along my torso. It felt so good to have her there, and I wanted nothing more than to claim her in every way.

But Levi's words echoed in my mind. We were on borrowed time.

On a gasp I tore my mouth away from hers. A new pain ricocheted through me, like a lightning strike, the urge to turn, to shift into something I'd never been…a beast.

"Do it," she urged.

As my body shuddered, on the cusp of transforming into a beast, I sunk my fangs into her throat, her blood coating my mouth and her pulse stroking my tongue.

Our bond snapped firmly into place. I felt her love, her power healing me.

This was it…everything I'd lived for.

I pulsed all my love, my conviction, my certainty that we were right to do this. I sent it all back to her.

Clothes came off with little concern for the damage we were doing. Time had stopped as far as I was concerned, and I needed to be inside my woman *now*.

"Kane," she moaned, and my name on her lips was music.

I cupped her face, staring into her eyes, and what pulsed between us closed all fissures in my heart and melded me to her so completely that it was like we were one.

She was panting, her breath coming in huffs, matching mine, our bodies slick with sweat. "Charlie," I whispered, reverent, in love.

She spread her legs wider, crossing them over my hips, and the heat of her pussy was too much to deny.

I thrust into her fully, claiming her as completely as she claimed me. Our bodies fused, the sensations like bombs exploding against every nerve ending, synapses firing. I was lost to her.

There would be time for wild, frenzied fucks, for whips and smacks, commands and the expectation of obedience. This? This was my time to love on her.

I rolled my hips, pushing deeper, rocking with her. She pressed her chest, nipples hard, teasing my skin. I slid my arms around her, bringing her closer so I could pump my cock, sink into her fully, claim her wholly and grip her face next to mine.

"You are my queen," I said into her ear. "And you are *mine*."

She murmured something that sounded like yes, her words lost to gasps as I thrust harder, faster, taking her with me as my climax roared. Coming inside Charlie was pure bliss, jetting into her, coating her, knowing it would drip out slowly later. I pushed her to her own orgasm, her pussy clenching tightly, squeezing everything I had and more.

I slowed my rocking, my hands back on her face, brushing her hair back from her sweaty cheeks. Her eyes were hooded, satisfaction buzzing between us.

"We'll have to do that again soon," she said, her voice lazy.

I nodded. "We have some business to take care of." As if I'd conjured trouble, the sound of shouts found our ears.

It was clear that Levi and Johnny were buying us time. I jumped to my feet, ready to pounce on anyone who came through the door.

Charlie touched my arm lightly. "You ready to fight?"

"At your side." I looked down at her. "Always."

Chapter Twenty-Three

Charlie

I burst through the door of my father's den as a beast, knowing that Sal had picked the location to hold Kane because of the narrow hallway leading to it.

The jolt of nostalgia had rocked me when I'd first arrived. The house itself was empty of occupants, which was odd enough to experience but the ghosts of everything I'd known and lost were still in the walls of the place.

Sal had changed the game and, I'd give him credit, he'd struck a nerve.

Despite the build-up, the only werewolves on the other side were mine — no sign of Sal or his pack. I stood huffing, Kane behind me fully healed and coming into his own version of a werebeast.

Levi and Johnny were still in human form, assessing the situation as their crews presumably worked through my childhood home.

"What the fuck?" Kane growled through his beastly muzzle.

"Sal's playing games. Magic everywhere." Levi turned to me. "He isn't on the premises, but he's making it seem like he is."

Just then a shadow figure moved at the end of the hall, low to the ground, like a wolf stalking. My instincts kicked into hyper drive. Hackles up, I was about to give change when Levi shook his head, a firm hand on my arm. "It's a trick. He's not here."

As if to prove his point, one of our pack came from the other side of the hall, diving for the movement, only to slam into the wall.

"So he's created a fun house." I should have known he'd make this as entertaining for himself as possible.

"Seems like it. The pack is encountering tricks of light, magical jolts, snares, all meant to keep them moving through the house." Levi pointed to the screen of his tablet. "They've made it through the top two floors, no casualties, but the higher you go, the sharper the deterrents. He wants us to stay down here."

"No, he'll want a chase. It'd be more fun if he keeps us moving down here...I'm guessing eventually to get us outside." I wanted to test the boundaries of the spell we'd ignited, but I knew by the sense of dread creeping along my skin and into my gut that we were trapped, not necessarily in the house but on the property — the last place I'd ever want to be stuck. A psychological mindfuck, thanks to my stepbrother. "Maybe we were thinking too literally about how he'd want to do that, though."

"The property isn't as vast as ours," Kane grumbled around his fangs as he looked over Levi's shoulder at his tablet. On it was the outline of my family home, dimensions of the land surrounding it.

"He's just getting started, I'm sure." The dread in my gut spread through my body. "Let's check things out."

A rumble rolled through the house, shaking it down to the foundation.

"What the—?"

The ground shook, knocking me sideways, and huge chunks of ceiling rained down.

Earthquake? *No.* This was magic. It scoured into my bones. My new powers narrowed my perception to a focus. Sal was orchestrating this spell, but he wasn't casting it. He had his witches with him, and they were just outside waiting for us to come running.

Instinct took hold. Fight turned to flight—but not the way Sal wanted. I shifted to wolf, knowing it'd be able to move quickly. My men followed me, and even Kane, so newly turned to werebeast, managed to control his new abilities and shifted to his wolf.

We ran one by one down the hall, diving out of the way of plaster, furniture toppling, paintings falling, glass breaking, raining down on us. The world shook, but I didn't know if it was concentrated to this house or beyond. The magic was everywhere, disorienting and sending pulses of artificial fear down my spine. It was clever, but I had protections now. I sent my own pulses down my threads, harnessing the power I now had, counteracting the effects of Sal's spells to the whole house. We wouldn't be tricked by his magic, no matter how strong. I'd make sure of it.

I knew the lay of the house, knew that at the end of this long hall we'd be faced with a choice. Left, to the back where the property yawned open—not inviting, for sure where Sal truly wanted me so he could start his hunt—or right, to the front foyer, which would only give us the option to travel deeper into the house.

Mayhem would be a guarantee. We'd be trapped, crushed by the house if Sal went that far. More likely, in for another round of fun and games.

Fuck that.

I growled, turned right, taking the men through the library where books were scattered all over the floor. The pack, our crew, were directly linked to my thoughts now that Kane and I were one. I strategized in the moment, sending them to other exits, ones Sal knew nothing about. Dad had built this place like a maze, full of hidden doors and secret tunnels. Sal was never patient enough to learn them, so even if he knew of their existence, he would never have traveled through them, not to mention that there were a few only I knew about. Dad had made sure of that.

I shifted to human, pulled down one of the books that remained standing and revealed a thick tunnel.

Just to be sure of my hunch, I took a deep breath, letting the smell of mildew and dust roll up my nose. There was no scent of wolf inside. It had stayed empty since the last time I had gone into it, which had been three years ago, the day I'd left my family home forever — or so I'd thought.

"This will take us outside but not the way Sal will be expecting." I waved the men to follow then shifted back to wolf. I ran into the darkness and through the layers of cobwebs, traveling down, the walls no longer shaking as badly, the concrete we'd descended too immune to Sal's wretched magic. We hit level ground. The scent of grass, scrubs, even a little bunny walloped my muzzle. I barreled through the last of the tunnel, crashing through the vines that covered its exit.

We burst out of the side of the house and into a labyrinth of bushes — the neglected rose maze my mother had loved, which was overgrown and unruly now. No one had dared touch it since her death.

I tested my own power, trying to see if I could crash through the boundaries that Sal's magic had cast. There was an invisible wall stretching the length of the property, along the fence at the edge of the maze that normally wouldn't have been a problem for us to breach in wolf form.

It was thick with Sal's nasty spell. The bond had ignited his devious plan, but that didn't mean he'd won.

I couldn't force my way through, so I'd use the boundaries to our advantage.

"Go. Lead the pack. Engage with Sal's crew. Buy me some time. I have an idea." I shot the idea out, my wolf thoughts focused, fully expecting my mates to understand.

"We aren't leaving you." Levi's voice boomed in my head, forceful while the others were silent. Johnny tossed his furry head into my side, nudging his agreement.

I shifted into a crouch, human once again but on all fours. "I need time," I whispered, feeling the edges of the magic that surrounded us. It ebbed through the bushes, reaching for me, urging me to run. I pushed against it, forcing it back, an internal battle that was all consuming. Sal wanted a hunt. I'd be damned if I gave him the one he expected.

Johnny nudged me again.

Levi was in my head. *"Charlie – "*

"I'm staying with her." Kane's voice came out of the darkness, a whip of a growl to punctuate. His huge furry foot came into my line of sight. "Go," he ordered.

I looked up at him, craning my neck. His body was all muscle, his chest heaving, eyes on fire, staring down on me with complete support, commitment shining at me while his beastly muzzle curled in a weirdly endearing smile.

There was no further discussion. Levi snorted, turned then ran.

Johnny, with a wolfie grin on his lips and one last nudge, chased after him. Not like my men didn't love the hunt, too.

Thank you, I pulsed to Kane, knowing that his alpha stance had saved me from a longer discussion. I appreciated my mates' concerns, their protection normally welcome, but it was more than I wanted right now. I knew he couldn't respond in a similar way, but his hand on my shoulder told me the message had been received.

I moved through the bush maze using the shadows to keep us concealed. The house stopped shaking at the same time that howls rent the night. I shivered as the clash of our pack against Sal's rolled over my body.

I needed to figure out a way to warp Sal's magic, to use it to my advantage.

I knew this land.

Vassa's words came back to me. *"What's your instinct telling you to do now? I bet it's telling you to step up, embrace the magic, trust it, let it do its thing."*

Lore and Sandro had gifted me a special kind of magic, true, but I also had what Levi had given me layered underneath—the ability to unravel what Sal's witches had done. I closed my eyes, tuned into all the threads from the connections I'd made, twining my new powers around them all. I had abilities, but I didn't have to wield them alone.

I pushed the intention out, gifting a fraction of what I had to the wolves under my command, including my mates.

I had to play the game that Sal started, just not according to his rules.

Howls echoed all around us, a shiver pricked over my skin as my pack embraced my offering then harnessed it to their use.

Kane shuddered behind me, no doubt feeling the effect of my power share more intensely.

I ran my hand along the tangled rose bushes, calling the natural magic around us, pulling it closer, using it to amplify the magic I had from Lore, from Sandro, from Levi. It mingled with the magic in the air, Sal's dirty spell, a magnetic pull to what was already around us. My stepbrother's magic tricks latched onto my own powers and instantly fell into my control. I laughed out loud, earning me a dark look from Kane.

My stepbrother had been such a fool. I mentally reached, pushing a bubble of Lupe magic out so it stuck to Sal's spells. Then, with a tremendous pull, I yanked harder, putting everything I had into severing the resistance until I'd wound his magic up with mine, like a web of glue. It hovered in the air, everywhere. I laughed again, *such a damn fool*, then pushed it out, sending my power as tendrils like snakes, searching for my target.

"Sal wants a hunt. I'm going to give him one."

Chapter Twenty-Four

Charlie

I'd wanted to battle Sal in the forest surrounding the Duke compound. I'd pegged it as the perfect location to end my stepbrother's grotesque thirst for murder. I'd spent hours building the space with magic, using the gifts I now had and the training Vassa had given me.

He'd changed the rules.

Now so had I.

I raced after my creatures, the magic that I'd created, hunters in their own right, seeking out my enemies.

Everything wolf in me loved the chase, sensing more than seeing the magic around us. Kane was at my back, on my heels — keeping up, staying alert.

I had fury. I had a taste for revenge. Sal would feel my wrath.

The witches casting a continuous spell were somewhere in the distance. The thump of their disembodied voices came at me from all sides. They'd detected I'd warped their magic and were battling back.

"*Levi*," I pulsed down our thread, "*find them.*" I felt him narrow his focus to the ones causing trouble.

I didn't need an affirmation to know he was on it.

Sal was nowhere and everywhere. I sensed him like a finger of ice down my spine. Whips of power from the desperate witches poked at me, urging me to run, to hide. I lashed them back, my wolfie ears picking up on their shrieks as one by one, Levi and his crew found them.

My father's property wasn't large, and it didn't provide a forest for cover or for hunting. What it had was a garden. Once cared for by my mother and adjacent by a few yards to the rose maze she'd built, this garden had every wonder that could grow in Vancouver and provided just enough twists and turns to make my snakes writhe in different directions on the search for Sal. I knew where he'd be, though.

My claws dug into the gravel and my paws skidded out from under me as I took a corner too fast. I rolled just in time to miss the shot of power that struck the bushes above my head.

I'd found Sal, his last witch by his side.

I sent a warning to Kane so he didn't attack head on, and we skirted the gazebo, keeping our bodies out of the line of witch fire. The snakes I'd made were losing their heads, blasted away by powerful spells, and I realized that this witch standing with my stepbrother was the only thing keeping my magic at bay.

I skidded in the dirt, changing direction as I assessed my brother and his ally, pushing away the pain of seeing this place, of being so near the last spot that I'd spend time with my mother. Sal knew how to wound me without using his teeth or his claws. That was the problem with blood family, they had all the weapons they needed to destroy a person from the inside out.

"Charlotte, you've surprised me." His voice was cocky as usual, but I detected a current of worry. "You've developed some new talents."

I didn't have time for conversation. Instead, I circled the gazebo, trying to find a weak point, pushing my power into every nook I could find, hoping that the witch at his side wasn't as powerful as she seemed.

The distant screams had stopped, and I sensed Levi and Johnny approaching cautiously. They had their crews with them, trailing at a distance.

"You may have found a way to counter my boundary spell, but you won't breach these protections." He made it sound like I should just give it up. I snorted as I passed Kane, who stayed rooted under the cover of a brush, hunkered down, his eyes locked on Sal, ready to attack at the slightest chance.

I pushed my powers out once again, putting all I had into coating the gazebo with the bubble of sticky shit that Sandro and Lore had gifted me. I felt the moment it locked into place, for once holding position like I actually knew what I was doing.

The vibe in the clearing altered, and the witch lost some of her ferocity. Her wild blonde curls stopped swirling around her head like a tornado and instead held on to the hint of a breeze like she was standing by the ocean instead of by my evil stepbrother. Her face, once contorted in magical frenzy was relaxed, her arms fell to her sides, her eyes lost their purpose.

Without me having to say a word, Levi shifted to human, walked into the clearing, pulling Sal's attention to the back of the gazebo. "What will you do, Sal? Stay in this little prison forever?"

Johnny took the other side, preferring to stay in wolf form as he trotted around the cobblestone walkway that surrounded the gazebo.

"Why are you letting them get so close!" Sal barked at his witch, then noticed finally that she had lost all will to obey. Before Sal could react, I found an opening where her magic had begun to fall away and jumped to the roof, skidding my claws along the tile, trying to get a hold. There was a loud slap from inside the gazebo then the witch inside murmured something, and the hole I thought I'd found in her magic closed.

"Kane, where are you hiding? I'd like to see your face while I destroy your mate." Sal sounded confident that he wasn't about to die. "The contract was signed. Even if I fail to get my chase tonight, it will happen. It's been written."

I jumped down, freeing myself from her spell.

Kane pushed himself from the cover I'd created for him to join his brothers as I raced around the perimeter, depositing my magic like land mines.

If I couldn't find a weakness, I'd make one.

"You've done everything I wanted you to do, Charlotte. You've fallen into every trap I've set for you." Sal mocked. "Now you're acting a fool, running around like you actually have a chance."

"We don't see it that way." Kane's voice held power. "What we see is a desperate coward confronted by wrath in the form of a queen."

Ignoring my mate, Sal continued with his end-of-life speech while I did what came naturally and followed Vassa's training. I was listening to my instincts.

"Your mother begged me not to kill her. She got on her knees and vowed she would obey me for the rest of her life if I'd only spare hers. She wanted to be able to protect you. She wanted to see you become this beast you have become." Sal's cruel laugh spurred me on. "I accepted her oath and demanded she tell me what your weakness was. She said the only weakness you had was your heart. She said, '*My daughter's love, her honor, her loyalty… It's the only thing you need to worry about.*' Such a silly thing. The love you held for your mother, your father, the Larsen clan, it truly was your weakness."

His words were blades, just as he knew they would be, my mother's last words being spoken to me so callously. I widened my circle around the gazebo, using my fury to ignite the spells I'd deposited, and my men, bless them, backed up too, sensing what was to come.

He was wrong… My mother wasn't telling him that my heart was my weakest point.

"I kept my end. I let her live as long as she obeyed me," Sal said. "I demanded she trade your life with hers. She refused. I ripped her throat out."

I shifted to beast, still moving the magic I had, rolling my monstrous arms so that I amassed a ball of power.

The witch's eyes widened as she took me in—horror quickly replacing the shock as I let my spell come to life, glowing with an iridescence that told her the truth. She was about to die. She screamed a warning that was seconds too late. My spells ignited as one, all directed at her, so her last noise was swallowed by a tower of flame. She was ash before Sal could even turn to look at her.

With the magic gone, Sal quickly assessed his situation. I could see the moment he realized he had to run, that he was going to be the one hunted.

Sal shifted to his wolf, the black beast who had murdered my mother and countless other female warriors. He bolted for the side opening, probably thinking I was too far away to reach him. As usual, he was just another male underestimating my power.

Two steps and one giant leap put me close enough to snatch him mid-jump. I had my murderer stepbrother by the scruff, and there was nothing he could do to fight me.

"No, you don't." I shook him, careless with his bones as I smashed his body against the stone pillars of the gazebo. Blood coated my fur, and for a moment, I had the compulsion to sink my fangs into his throat and mark him as mine...to rule over him so he would forever know what it was like to be forced to obey.

I shuddered.

Even the thought of that was too disgusting to dwell on long.

"My mother didn't tell you my weakness, you fool." I growled, taking a page out of his book. "She told you to be worried about my loyalty." I slammed his body against the ground, sweeping him back up so his black eyes were staring into mine. "My honor." I snatched his throat with my other hand. "And my love." I dug my claws into the back of his neck. "You should have listened to her."

I showed him my fangs, let reality set in and fear finally shine in his eyes then I ripped into his furry throat, his foul blood coating my tongue for a second before I tore myself away, spat the gore to the ground then locked eyes with him once again.

Terror shone back at me, life drained quickly and I held Sal up, keeping him in my sight then smiled.

"You lose."

Chapter Twenty-Five

You all belong to me, and I belong to you. Finally, we are complete.

The tendrils of ether in my shadow world circle us, three virile men and me, a lusty, very spoiled, female.

You close the space between us, your grip firm on the back of my neck, commanding as you tilt my head to stare down at me. Your lava eyes blaze with love, heating me down to my toes.

You kiss me with fire, sparks flying over my skin as other hands caress my tits, my ass. Someone parts my thighs, stroking flames along my skin.

I arch into your touch, giving myself over to your desire while burning through my own.

I called to you while I slept, but waking doesn't stop our entanglement. We were on our shared bed, extra-large mattress to accommodate my big men. The fight was over, for now. We'd conquered the immediate evil and rid the world of a wolf killer.

Now was the time for our bonds to cure, to work out our kinks and know each other more intimately than ourselves.

For me, this was the best part.

Johnny was between my legs, sucking on my pussy like a man starved. Kane's hands caressed my cheeks, holding me in a never-ending kiss that obliterated my soul each second that passed.

Levi attended to my nipples, plucking relentlessly, making me writhe.

I reached blindly, one hand traveling down Kane's torso until I gripped his shaft while with the other hand, I did the same to Levi. Two cocks in my fists, coordinating became a feat in concentration. I knew by the moans that I was doing something right.

My insides coiled, orgasm building, pleasure a tight spiral that twisted and turned. Johnny slipped his fingers into my hole, rubbing deeply, forcefully, against my G-spot.

Kane pulled away but only to shift closer, to replace his lips with his cock. My mouth stretched beyond comprehension, but I took him in, savoring the salty tang of his pre-cum and the burn of my lips spread wide. He rubbed my jaw tenderly, coaxing me to unhinge, to take him down. I swallowed him whole, and he eased slowly until he was seated right down to the base.

I cupped his balls, kneaded them gently and was rewarded by another groan.

I stroked the tip of Levi's dick, rubbing moisture down his head, over the ridge, along his shaft.

I was bombarded by sensation, my climax taut, ready to give. I don't know how I lived before this — three men, all devoted to making me feel it all.

Johnny stopped what he was doing, and I wanted to protest, but I had a dick in my mouth stopping me from saying a word.

Kane moved slowly, pumping out enough to bring his tip to my lips, then back again. Johnny slipped his cock into my pussy, pinioning me, making me mew around Kane's dick.

Three cocks winding me up. Three men making me quiver and shake. My orgasm exploded through me. My legs fell open wider than before, and my back arched, pushing my tits against Levi's lips. Kane's dick slipped in and out, and I pressed my tongue to the ridges of his cock.

Johnny came first, filling me up with hot jets as he fiercely pumped my pussy.

Kane came next, drilling my mouth as his cum flowed down my throat, searing me with his heat right down to my core.

Levi spurted his cum all over my tits, coating my skin in his passion, scalding my skin deliciously.

My imagination could never conjure this much pleasure. To be satiated by three men who owned my heart was never part of my plans. But now, somehow, it was part of my future.

We wrung each other dry, coaxing every last shudder until we collapsed, entangled limbs, cocks, semi-hard, gearing up for another go, all of us sweaty, cum-coated and satiated…if only for the moment.

This was lust and love, family and friends, bonded as one. The sorrow that had ripped my heart to pieces years ago was a whisper, and my heart healed, patchwork by these men, by the packs of wolves I governed, the loyalty that I commanded.

I was to be queen, savior of the female wolves — and no one would stop me.

Want to see more from this author? Here's a taster for you to enjoy!

Trouble With Cats
Angela Addams

Excerpt

Crimson

Crimson had picked her hiding place carefully — downwind, in the shadows and under a heaping arch of brush, deep in the forest where she knew at least one of her stalkers wouldn't find her. The advantage of being on foot was that she could slip quickly under the trees' canopy, obscuring the eagle-eyed vision of Talon, whose shrill cry overhead made her smirk. He was frustrated, to be sure. This game had gone on longer than he'd wanted.

The echoing crack of a branch underfoot had her crouching lower, her breath barely there as she reined in the urge to bolt. A predatory snort, closer than she'd like, had her heart pounding so thunderously that she was sure she'd give herself up any second.

Unlike the eagle shifter, in his wolf form, Valor would have no trouble hunting her at ground level. The only thing she had going for her was her head start and how easily she'd wedged herself under the protection of the piled branches. If she was lucky, he wouldn't be able to pick up her scent.

With the way she was sweating, though, she'd probably need to shift to plan B shortly.

Another snort, another twig creaking. Normally he wouldn't be so noisy, but she guessed he wanted her to know he was near. He wanted her to know that her little game was becoming tedious and that she would pay, one way or another. Still she hunkered down, holding her breath now that he was so close, determined to win this round, at least. Through the thicket, a flash of gray fur strode by — so leisurely, so assured. As an apex predator in Shade, he was monstrously large, as were all the familiars, but Valor also had an air of sophistication along with his brute force, as though he were a king among his kind, even when he, along with Crimson and Talon, was an outcast.

She loved that about him.

Crimson's lungs, pushed to their limit of air deprivation, wheezed out a short gasp through her clenched lips. She froze, scanning the small area in her line of sight. It was hardly a sound, and yet...

The ground beneath her shook with the thundering approach of Valor. She had an easy escape route, but she waited, pushing down the instinct to get out and run. She didn't know which direction he was coming from, but she knew it was only a matter of time before—

The stacked branches around her creaked and groaned, threatening to collapse with her underneath as Valor pounced on top of her hiding spot. She rolled to the side and briefly made eye contact with the beast. His cunning brown gaze shone with triumph.

Not yet, wolfie. Not yet.

He shoved his snout between two branches and wedged one paw, claws out, through the wood. Crimson grinned.

"Gotcha." She kicked as hard as she could, and as the entire structure began to fall, entangling the wolf in an avalanche of debris, she rolled out of the way, clearing the mess before Valor even knew what had happened. She was on her feet, bolting to the tree line, keeping her snickers contained as much as she could as she listened to Valor's grunts and huffs behind her. He was too big to get out of the disaster of branches gracefully.

The barn was a short distance from the forest—the closest point of safety—which was why she'd chosen the hiding spot she had. She paused only briefly to look up at the sky. The summer sun was at its peak, beating down relentlessly, despite the veil of fog that Crimson had built around her safe haven. She scanned the skies again but there was no sign of Talon. Almost out of breath, her chest heaving, she made a dash for it, pumping her legs as hard as she could. All she needed was two minutes. Two minutes and she'd win.

Talon's screech sounded like fury itself, and Crimson dug deep, pushing harder toward her goal.

Fifty feet.

Forty.

Thirty.

She dared not look up or behind. She didn't need to anyway, because she felt the predators closing in. They were at her heels and above her head.

Twenty feet remaining.

She would make it this time.

She would—

One foot landed wrong, and instead of touching the wood of the barn, she face-planted right into the grass.

Oof!

Dirt rammed against her face and embedded into her hair. Bits of grass flew up her nose. She coughed and sneezed, too disoriented and out of breath to do much more than accept defeat.

Valor howled seconds before skidding over her, his giant paws caging her head while the rest of him pressed into her body. She pushed herself up—or tried to, anyway—just as Talon landed, his claws digging into the ground in front of her. Valor shoved her down with his snout between her shoulder blades. Talen dropped rope with two loops for her wrists in front of her face.

"Yeah, yeah." She spat dirt then slipped her hands through the loops.

Valor prodded her roughly, giving her enough space so she could flip over. He was grinning like a crazy wolf, his fangs bared and muzzle scrunched.

"Rub it in, why don't you?"

The rope loops tightened as Talon took flight, the force of his ascent whipping her to her feet in seconds. She stumbled backward until her shoulders pressed against the wall of the barn, her toes barely touching the ground. The rope pulled taut, letting her know that Talon had secured her. She was trapped and at the mercy of her familiars...again. Talon's cry sounded like victory. She looked up to see him circle above, letting her know what she had coming.

She kept losing this game. On purpose? No, she was too competitive for that, and yet, something always seemed to cause her to trip up at the last minute.

"You're a terrible hider, Crimson." Valor's voice rumbled like thunder, forcing her attention to him.

She pulled her gaze from Talon to see that Valor was fully clothed still, which was hardly like him at a time like this. All the same, the tight breeches he liked to wear left very little to the imagination—not that she minded. She enjoyed seeing how aroused her men got, even if it was hidden behind their clothes temporarily. His loose-fitting shirt was unbuttoned enough to give her a glimpse of the dark curls of chest hair that she loved feeling pressed against her skin, roughly warming her with every thrust. He ran his fingers through his hair, then shook the curls out, a gesture that made him look like he had no cares in the world when they both knew he was dying to fuck her silly.

She knew this for certain because her men always wanted to fuck her silly, but also because his cock strained against his pants like it was ready to burst out on its own.

What she wouldn't give to swallow him whole. To taste his cum. To lick his balls.

She squirmed, lust pooling in her every erogenous zone.

"Growing impatient, darling?" Talon spoke as he shifted, a unique talent that few familiars had.

"A taste of her own medicine, I'd say," Valor added.

"You two wouldn't have caught me if I hadn't stumbled." Crimson tugged on the ropes, even though she knew it was pointless. She could use her power to get herself out of the bindings at any time but where was the fun in that?

"Stumbled?" Valor laughed. "Is that what that was?"

"Looked more like eating dirt to me." Talon swooped in to run his fingers over her cheek, his golden eyes sparkling. "In fact, you've got some grass right here."

She flicked her cheek to the side in a vain attempt to shift away from him. He gripped her chin in response and yanked her face toward him again, all playfulness gone from his eyes. "Now, now, Crimson, no need to be a sore loser."

"I'm not a sore—"

He cut off her words with a kiss—a demanding, tongue-probing, toe-curling kiss. She melted. How could she not? Talon was not only a fierce protector and loyal familiar, but he loved her and made sure she knew it in every imitate moment they shared.

He released her too soon, turning her chin to the side. Her protest was cut short by Valor and his teasing kiss—a nip on her bottom lip, a soothing lick, then a leisurely stroking that incinerated her every last urge to resist.

Why would she, anyway? This was what she wanted—to be bound and at the mercy of her men.

Talon draped a rough swath of fabric over her eyes then tied it so tightly behind her head that she gasped. Valor nipped her bottom lip one last time before pulling away. She tugged on her arms as if she could coax him back with a touch, but the binding was too strong for her to move more than an inch away from the wall, so she only managed to make herself sway. Someone tugged another piece of cloth over her mouth, slipping it between her lips so that her jaw was wedged slightly open and her lips pulled taut.

She'd put her war gear on for their game, which meant the men had to navigate a series of buttons and hooks to unravel the layers of skintight fabric that wrapped around Crimson's body. *Hardly a challenge for these two.*

They had her stripped bare in a matter of moments. The sun's heat beat down on her exposed skin so she was slick with sweat. A wisp of a breeze, full of grass and dirt and the heady scent of her familiars' arousal was like a balm, making her nipples harden to the point of aching need. She loved fucking these men in the middle of the day, outside, without a care as to who might see.

Not that anyone visited their little hideaway. They'd all been banished a year ago, forgotten by the court in place of a death sentence for a crime she hadn't committed.

It was meant to be a punishment, but really it was a blessing — peace, quiet, the never-ending roll of days with nothing to do.

At least, that's what she told herself.

Hands cupped her breasts. Fingers splayed her pussy lips. A tongue traced the side of her neck. Sensations of exquisite torture, teasing touches, barely-there kisses… Someone hauled her ass up with strong hands, cupping her cheeks. Hot breath cascaded over her clit.

Anticipation made her squirm.

Desire and need coiled deep inside her core, every muscle tight, waiting for release.

Someone covered her nipple with hot, wet heat and a flickering tongue. Someone squeezed her other breast to the point of pain. Her men both had large hands and big mouths, wide enough to envelop her tits almost completely, which made it impossible to know who was playing with what. But that didn't matter, because her body was on fire. Every nerve-ending jolted as her lust wound around the pinnacle of release.

A flick of her clit made her moan behind the gag. The hands on her ass hoisted her higher, a feast on display as thumbs yanked her pussy open wider. A strong, determined tongue roughly licked her from top to bottom so that rolling waves of nearly unbearable pleasure made her whimper and groan. Finally, lips latched onto her clit with force and huge fingers thrust inside, seeking that special rhythm so that the bud of her G-spot roared to life.

Featherlight kisses just below her earlobe made her shiver.

Relentless pounding of thick fingers in her pussy made her gasp.

The coil of her climax tightened with each nip and flick and suck of her nipples.

She writhed and swayed and desperately wanted to pull away from the intensity, but instead her body pleaded for *moremoremore*.

When her orgasm crested, it was a rising peak that seemed to stretch beyond the sky. She held back for as long as she could, reveling in the waves of power that built it higher and higher. Her breath caught. Her body froze. She was on the edge with a sheer drop seconds away.

One more flick.

One more suck.

One more kiss.

She arched into the dive, her body contorting and rolling and spasming. Her synapses fired all at once then short-circuited with the bombardment of sensations. Light exploded behind her eyes as she rode the wave through every pulse-pounding, pussy-quivering second of it.

Her men didn't let her go — not even when her legs shook, not even when she moaned from the pit of her desire. They were relentless, caressing every tiny bit of pleasure out of her until she was limp, out of breath and complete putty.

Someone untied her arms so she could collapse properly into his arms. By the way he kissed her, so sweetly, she knew it was Talon who cradled her. It was

Valor, then, who undid the gag, then the blindfold. She kept her eyes closed to protect against the blinding sun.

"Time for a bath, Crimson. You're a mess." Talon's voice was a gruff command. No debate. He loved to bathe her, and she loved the way he worshipped her body, so he'd get no resistance from her — not that she could move of her own volition right now anyway.

She blinked her eyes open to smile at Valor, who was only a step behind her.

She expected to see the cocky smirk of a job well done, so when his beautiful face twisted into a pain-filled grimace, Crimson jolted and a knot tightened in her gut.

Talon's next step landed wrong, and instead of carrying her forward, he began to fall. He curled himself around her body, clearly trying to protect her from hitting the ground, even though his arms shook and tears streamed from his eyes. He rolled so she landed on top of him, bearing the brunt of a hard landing on his shoulders and back.

"What's wrong?" Crimson split her attention between her familiars.

Valor clenched his chest, like his heart was about to burst from his flesh. She felt Talon's body vibrating beneath her fingers, his pulse probably racing at the same pace as Valor's.

Valor's eyes flashed between wolf and human, taking on a predatory gleam as he struggled to stop himself from shifting.

She moved off Talon's body just as he contorted then rolled into a ball, holding his gut, moaning in obvious agony.

"Something's wrong—" Valor sputtered. "Can't keep hold—"

"No shit!" Crimson grounded herself, connecting with the natural magic of the earth while at the same time yanking her magic from its resting place. Her familiar marks flared in hues of red, coursing power from her toes to her scalp. She put one hand on Valor, one on Talon, hoping to tap into whatever was causing them pain so she could obliterate it. As soon as she laid her hands on them, she flew back like she'd touched a lightning bolt. Searing pain roared through her body, tearing over her from sternum to groin. It felt like her head was splitting, her limbs ripping from their sockets...

Death. Death was all around them...in them, taking violently from somewhere. Echoed screams ricocheted through her conscious mind, and she knew... She just knew.

My sister...one of three witches in the Court of Shade—a triad that maintained balance in their world. *My sister is dead.*

"Aria—" Crimson gasped.

Talon, now in his eagle form, took flight with a screeching wail. Valor, now a wolf, limped toward her.

They'd been forced to shift, and the only thing that could do that was the death of one of their own. A Brother of Shade had died and so had her sister.

Their sanctuary. Their blessing. It all shattered.

Crimson didn't know who the enemy was, but she knew her peaceful days were over.

About the Author

Angela Addams is an author of many naughty things. She believes that the written word is an amazing tool for crafting the most erotic of scenarios and likes telling stories about normal people getting down and dirty and falling in love. Enthralled by the paranormal at an early age, Angela also spends a lot of her time thinking up new story ideas that involve supernatural creatures in everyday situations.

She is an avid tattoo collector, a total book hoarder, and loves anything covered in chocolate…except for bugs. She lives in Ontario, Canada in an old, creaky house, with her husband, children and four moody cats.

Angela loves to hear from readers. You can find her contact information, website details and author profile page at https://www.firstforromance.com

Home of Erotic Romance

Sign up for our newsletter and find out about all our romance book releases, eBook sales and promotions, sneak peeks and FREE romance books!